STERLING

MIRANDA LYNN

Welcome to the
pack darlin!

Miranda
Lynn

OTHER BOOKS BY MIRANDA LYNN

Destiny Finds Her
Blair's Destiny

BLACK MOUNTAIN PACK
Mack
Rook

ACKNOWLEDGEMENTS

FIRST OF ALL I want to thank my readers for continuing to stick with me on this writing journey of mine. For loving my Pack as much as I do.

I want to thank my editor, Ansley Blackstock, for being there and helping me polish Sterling's story to be the best it can be. Our relationship gets better with each book we work on.

My beta readers for catching the little things that slip past all the other eyes that have seen this story.

To Angie Stanton and Kelly Solomon for being there on short notice to help read through sections, and always being the first in line for ARC copies. Thank you for loving my guys and gals as much as I do.

To Sandra and JM, girls, you were there when I was faltering and doubting myself. Thank you for your support, your positive words, and for just being the awesome women and authors that you are.

PROLOGUE

Welcome to the Black Mountain Pack

OUR PACK WAS created over fifty years ago for the sole purpose of helping the shifter species survive. When we as shifters came out of the shadows and admitted what and who we were to the humans, our dream of living together in peace went down the shitter. Instead, fear ruled, and all shifters were hunted to near extinction. Our life of peace was gone and our days filled with anxiety. Never sure who we could trust. If it weren't for Jerome, his forward thinking, and the assistance of his affluent, still in the closet shifter friend Leo, we would probably all be dead. Now, after years of trial and error, we have learned to live together in peace. Different species banded together in each pack or pride, and have proven we aren't the threat most humans thought us to be.

Jerome, the Alpha of the Black Mountain Pack, mated a Panther we rescued, and we, the pack as a whole, adopted her son Mack. He has raised him and groomed him for an Alpha role himself. Jerome also helped many find a welcome home, taking in stranded cubs. One little girl grabbed his heart, but was quickly taken from us during a raid. He and Mack spent years searching for her. Mack thought he was just bringing his sister back home when he finally found her, but fate had other plans. Casey wasn't destined to be his sister, but his mate. We unanimously chose to help defeat her biological father, a deranged panther Alpha from the South American jungle. Jerome declared Casey the victor, the first female Alpha in Shifter history.

For safety reasons Rook, who joined our pack when Casey was first adopted, travelled to South America to make sure the pride there was safe for her arrival. Rook revealed to us that he had been Casey's guard in the pride before her mom escaped to America with her. Casey was the only reason he had stayed in that pride, she wormed her way into his heart from the moment he met her. He had lost their trail, and rather than return to the pride had sought refuge with Jerome, and secretly searched for her. He stepped up and volunteered to return to the pride as Casey's interim Alpha while she learned all she could from Mack and Jerome.

Rook found more than he planned upon arrival. A broken pride filled with damaged members, his mate among them. Proof that fate's plans are always in the works. Jazz has been a great asset to both pack and pride.

Marla, my right-hand gal at the bar, and Jax, our pack healer who works in the human world as an EMT, traveled down to help, and after a grueling extended stay, Marla returned with two cubs in tow. Surprising the hell out of everyone in the pride. Especially me, it hurt a bit to know she didn't trust me enough to confide in me about them. She currently lives above the bar in the small apartment with both of them. A little female minx and a male fox who are devious little buggers.

Rook and Jazz came back shortly after to continue Jazz's therapy and bring her into the loving fold of the pack. They have made progress in their relationship but have a long way to go before she is fully free of the demons haunting her.

Now Mack and Casey are successfully leading a growing pride on its way to a healthy existence. Along with raising newborn twins of their own.

All the while I stayed here manning my bar and watching out for the pack I helped Jerome create half a century ago. Though the itch to move on has become like a never-ending flea bite. My loyalty is to Jerome, so I'll ignore that need for a bit longer. With all the changes that have occurred the makeup of the bar employees need a change. With two cubs to take care of Marla requires more conventional schedule, though she doesn't realize it yet. Working nights and living above a bar isn't the best for a family. Suzanne, the Alpha's wife, is more than happy to help care for the cubs while Marla works, but those little ones desire a stable home and parental figure.

As word of these changes have traveled we have seen a rise in applicants to the pack. There are four potential members I think will work well at the bar. I was preparing to discuss them with the Alpha when I received a call from Leo, a shifter we hadn't heard from since Jerome requested his assistance for Rook in South America. His request put a challenging spin on things. Our time of complacency as a pack is over. The world is changing, and with that brings renewed opposition, and a hunger for power among not only shifters, but the whole supernatural community.

CHAPTER 1

REANA

THE ACRIDITY OF burnt flesh assaulted my nose.

The screeching of rubber and clanging of metal crushing against metal vibrated in my ears.

The flames burned a permanent tattoo on my retinas.

I stood slack jawed and unbelieving at the sight before me. The whole crash happened in seconds, but played out in slow motion over and over in my head. Orchestrated by the lone figure, draped in black, still standing in the middle of the road. I snuck back in my building to avoid being seen. My heart racing, breaths short, and tears streaming down my face. My best friend, the woman who had been my roommate since I had joined the pack, and her fate-chosen mate had just been eliminated with no regard to who saw.

ONE HOUR EARLIER

Tammy burst through the door of our

apartment. "I need to pack, Rea, help me." She was bouncing with excitement, flitting around grabbing things.

"Why? What's the hurry?" I followed her to our room. Our apartment was part of our "benefit" package while working at the club. Ours was small, a single bedroom shared by two women who became best friends on sight. Located in a dingy building in the seedy part of town, the only comfort was the security the pack provided making it the safe haven it had become.

"Ricky said yes. He released me from my contract so I can be with Jerry. I'm moving in with him tonight!"

"Are you serious? Slow down, wait." I trailed her as she threw random things in her bag. What she said didn't make sense, no one had ever been released from their contract. Especially not to be with a mate. Ricky wasn't the Alpha last time I checked, he was just the manager of the club. Jacob was our Alpha, and had been for the past five years. He had proven himself when he challenged for the position. He was a strong and fearless wolf that led with both his head and his heart. No one had been strong enough to defeat him since. I was extremely confused. I grabbed her arm to get her attention.

"What exactly did he say?'

She huffed out a breath at my hand. "He said if that is your choice, to be with a mate, then leave. I release you."

"Release you from what?" I asked, while trying to decipher how he had worded it.

"My contract, silly." She tugged away and continued stuffing clothes and odds and ends into her bag and moved to our bathroom. "Jerry is on his way to get me. His granddad left him a cabin on the edge of town, and we are going to make that our home. Tonight we complete our mating." She popped her head out the door. "Rea, I am so ready."

"Tammy, I hate to break it to you, but our contracts aren't with Ricky. He just manages the club for Jacob."

"They are now, Rea. He's the new Alpha, didn't you know? The shift happened this morning, you were probably sleeping. He defeated Jacob in one on one combat."

I wandered into the living room while she finished in the bathroom. I retreated back into my head feeling for the pack bond that kept me connected to the other members. I found the web. It used to be shiny silvery threads connecting all the members, but now there was a dark slimy residue on a lot of them. The thicker strand indicating the Alpha was coated in tar that hadn't been there before. It was tightly wound and led to Ricky declaring that he was our new leader. The sludge coating the threads pulsed giving off small waves of darkness. I backed out quickly and mentally built a wall between myself and the web, only allowing my still shining thread to penetrate.

"Tammy, look at the bonds. Something isn't right."

"It's fine, Rea, you worry too much." Tammy made it the four short steps to the living room slash kitchen where I was standing. "Can't you just be happy for me? I finally get my happy ever after. A mate, and babies soon, I hope." She blushed slightly. "Stop worrying this one time and just be happy for me."

I sighed knowing no matter what I said Tammy would still leave. "I am, Tam, I just worry about you. Please be careful."

"We will. Come downstairs with me? Jerry should be here soon; I don't want him waiting on me."

"Of course." Even with her faults I loved Tammy, and really wanted to see her happy. She could be stubborn when she wanted to as well, and this was one of those times. It wouldn't matter what I said, or what I could prove, she was going through with leaving.

We waited about ten minutes, and I prayed the whole time to the gods, goddesses, whoever looked over us to keep them safe, to make what Tam said true, and not a twisted way for Ricky to be able to come after them and eliminate them. That my worries would be for nothing. As I was finishing the rumble of Jerry's Mustang announced his arrival. My gut clenched when he pulled up, dread weighing my shoulders down. Instinct told me this would be the last time I would see Tammy, and there wasn't a damn thing I could do about it.

Jerry loaded her bags in the car as she hugged me one last time.

"Please be careful, Tam, have him drive straight to the cabin, ok?" I begged her, tears building in my eyes.

"Rea, we will be fine. Stop worrying."

Jerry stood holding her door open as she sank into the leather seat. She waved at me again through the window as he rounded the hood to take his place behind the wheel. The engine roared to life and he squealed the tires as they took off and drove straight to their death.

CHAPTER 2

STERLING

THE ANNOYING LYRICS of "What Did the Fox Say" invaded my much loved cycle of sleep. I cracked an eye open ready to tear someone a new asshole until I realize the music was coming from my own phone. *Son of a bitch.*

"Damn cubs," I muttered as I drug myself into an upright position and grab the phone silencing it without even glancing at the caller ID. Whoever it is could call back after I've had my first cup of java.

Rubbing the sleep from my eyes I glanced around to orient myself. Once again I had opted to crash in my office after closing time rather than journey the five miles home. I had been spending more nights at the bar than at my place. My fox and I were becoming more restless, with a need I couldn't define. I just know that he wanted to move, explore. That persistent need increased with each passing day, like a flea bite I couldn't reach.

The screen on my phone lit up as that damn song rang out again. I decided the office had new rules starting that day—Marla could not bring the cubs to work again. Ever since she brought them back from South America they had taken to technology like a fish takes to water, and they both loved playing tricks on me. This was the last straw. I silenced it again without checking the screen. Immediately the phone on my desk began to ring, and I knew if I didn't answer I wouldn't get any peace this morning.

"Yeah," I said into the receiver, the sleep hanging on in the gruffness of my voice.

"About damn time you answered." I recognized Leo's growly bass. "There's a situation. I need you." He was a man of few words.

"When?"

"Yesterday. Meet me in an hour at Jerome's."

"Ten-four." I hung up. Leo didn't trust anything but face to face communication for important shifter business. I brewed a mug of coffee, and grabbed a change of clothes from my bag in the corner. I had plenty of time since Jerome's house was only ten minutes away if I drove the speed limit, five minutes by my bike. Leo would take the tunnels he had created when the house was built that connected his office building downtown straight to the Alpha's house.

I took a few moments to enjoy my coffee and think on how things have changed recently. The pack had grown so much since that time, and no matter how hard we tried to talk Leo into joining officially he still chose to be a loner, hiding his true nature from the world. Staying an anonymous player up in his glass tower. We could always depend on him for help outside the pack abilities, and his loyalty never strayed.

This past year brought the most change and Leo stepped up when the need arose. Between Mack finding out his long lost adopted sister was actually his mate, to helping the pack fight her maniacal father. He jumped in when supplies and medical assistance were needed by Rook in South America before Casey could take her place as the first female Alpha of a pride. That was one fucked up situation. Leo took it in stride and provided transportation, and searched the shifter world finding the best therapist in the world. He flew her in to help Rook's mate and all the females and cubs begin to work through the years of damage that Casey's father had inflicted upon them. Leo was always there to help us work outside the box.

Mack and Casey are building the South American Pride back to its glory, and Rook and Jazz travel between the pack and pride assisting where they can. This travel is part of Jasmine's therapy. She is helping to build a center for the pride members who need ongoing therapy and lifetime support.

I glanced at the clock on my phone and realized I needed to get a move on to make the meeting. I grabbed the folder sitting on my desk that held the applications for four potential pack members that I wanted to have approved and directed to work in the bar. Marla needed more hands to cover shifts now that she had the cubs. I wanted her to have the freedom of a day job, and I have been itching to travel, but with the responsibilities I still held with my bar I couldn't do that. Giving her the title of manager would allow me to pass most of those to her and free me up to travel. I am happy that our pack is growing and mates are being found, but it increased the longing I had for a mate of my own again. I knew I wasn't as lucky as Jerome, who got a second chance at love with a mate. No other mates were out there for me.

Maybe this meeting with Leo would provide just the change I needed. I headed out to Jerome's with renewed excitement at the adventure ahead.

CHAPTER 3

*J*EROME OPENED THE door before I could knock. The sound of laughter flowed out and embraced me. That sound had been absent from our pack for too long. "Come on in, Sterling." He motioned for me to follow him to his office. Squeals chased us down the hall. "We won't be disturbed in here."

Jerome's office was soundproof. Dark wood covered the walls and a large desk took up most of the space. Two large leather chairs faced it, with a picture window behind the desk and one off to the right that allowed the Alpha to monitor the grounds. The windows were deeply tinted and bulletproof. The walls were covered with floor to ceiling bookshelves full of leather-bound tomes. Many covering the history of shifters, the wars, the hunts, and more recently the changes that have allowed us to survive. Everything was large and overstuffed matching the large wolf that sat before me.

"Sounds like the cubs are settled just fine," I commented as I took a seat.

He smiled. "Yes, but some days I miss the quiet. Suzanne loves the chaos though. She spoils those cubs rotten. Rook and Jazz have been a great help, but I think it's time they focused on growing their bond without distraction." Jerome laughed. "I've begun construction on a home for them, it should be finished within the month. Now if Marla would just agree to move to the lands as well." He sighed, leaving that statement unfinished.

"Ah, I think I may have a solution for that. Did you get the applications I sent?"

Jerome opened a folder on his desk and pulled out four packets. "I have, and I agree with you that they would all be assets. What is your plan? You know Marla won't take well to being forced into another position."

"Agreed. That's why I want to ask her to take over management of the Silver Fox." I sat straighter as I let that sink in.

"But the bar is your baby." Jerome sputtered in surprise, quirking an eyebrow. "I never thought you would give the reins to another." He was cut off by a knock behind one of the bookcases.

I watched, as at the push of a button the bookcase swung out, and Leo walked in.

"Well, that's handy." I smiled and rose

to shake Leo's outstretched hand. He nodded at Jerome in greeting and took the chair next to me.

"You have confirmed everything?" Jerome asked. His demeanor changed from jovial friend to assertive Alpha.

"One hundred percent," Leo replied, and angled toward me. "Sterling, I have been made aware of a rough situation with a pack in Texas, and I need a team to go in and try to assess things from the inside. I need your help."

"My help? How?" I couldn't imagine with the connections he had why Leo would need the help of a bar owner.

"You are perfect for the cover I have developed. I was approached by the former Alpha of this pack asking for assistance with his club. He wanted me to become an investor and help him turn the club into a thriving meeting place for everyone in the supernatural world. I had considered it, but my contact in the pack called this morning, and the chain of command has changed for the worse. There is much more going on, and my source has confirmed that this club is just a front to build resources for the rebel group calling themselves "The Resistance.""

My Fox growled at that declaration. Leo,

Jerome, and I had battled this faction before, and had believed it to be dead. I looked at Jerome who didn't seem surprised by this revelation. "Did you know?"

"Yes, he contacted me a week ago with his initial idea and asked my permission to recruit you." He sighed. "As much as I wanted to say no, I couldn't. Your life is yours, and I won't keep you where you don't want to be. But know that his proposition comes with dangers we haven't yet faced."

"So you know about the return of The Resistance. Then you should know I can't sit back and allow another pack to be victimized again. All supernatural beings should be given the chance to have the freedom we enjoy."

"I agree, I just hate that you feel you have to be the one to bring it around. Leo can be very persuasive and evasive at the same time. I just want you to go into this with your eyes wide open."

"Jerome, with your permission I want to help Leo." I stood and strode to the window that overlooked the side yard where the cubs were playing with Jazz. "The pack is growing and changing and I am thankful for that, but I feel my place here isn't as important as it used to be. I'm ready to move on and start helping outside the pack.'

"Sterling, you will always be needed. You and I started this pack, you are as much a part of it as I am." Jerome leaned forward, realization in his eyes. "The matings are affecting you, aren't they?"

"They are, Jerome, I may just be a fox, but I'm a sly one, and a lonely one." I smiled.

"Very well, if you can get Marla to agree, and have the bar taken care of, you have my permission to go." Jerome stood.

Leo smiled. "Great. I'll have Wyatt contact you with the details." He rose and slipped out the way he had come in.

I walked over and grasped Jerome's hand, pulling him into a hug. This wasn't a choice I was making lightly. "I'll have everything set before I leave. Do you want to contact the applicants or should I?"

"I'll call them with approval, and have each of them meet you this afternoon at the bar."

"Sounds good."

I left the main house with a renewed sense of purpose. Knowing that I had Jerome's support meant the world to me.

CHAPTER 4

I *PARKED MY BIKE* next to the back door to the bar. I wasn't looking forward to the discussion I needed to have with Marla. As a fox shifter confrontation wasn't a favorite of ours, especially when dealing with a more predatory shifter. We had always gotten along because I gave her the freedom to run things as she saw fit. Most days she was good at what she does, and in the pack she was more submissive than some. Still, as a lynx she felt the urge to dominate my fox at times, being in charge of the bar alleviated that, allowing us to live in the pack without confrontation. I had elevated to my status in the pack more from my human nature and experience than my animal side. I took a deep breath and headed inside.

Jake, who had become our full time cook, was already in the kitchen preparing tonight's special. He greeted me with a nod of his head, his hands deep in some type of dough. He was a wonder with food, and enjoyed cooking when between missions. He had been the one to find Casey years ago, and had protected her until her shifter side emerged again. When that happened his job was done and he came to work for me full time. Even with Marla's mood swings he'd rather be here than anywhere else.

"Have you seen Marla?" I could sniff her out, but with all the scent layers in the bar it was faster to just ask.

"She's out front doing inventory," he replied.

I strode through the swinging door to find her. The tables gleamed which meant she had spent the day doing a thorough scrubbing. The floors even shined a bit, and I hadn't seen them shine in years. Not a good sign. She cleaned like this when she was pissed. I took a moment to appreciate the room before me. I built this as a haven for shifters many years ago—even through the bar fights, economic downswing, and initial trepidation that the local humans had toward shifters, she still stands strong. I kept things to a minimum on decor. Deep burgundy seats surrounded each mahogany table, a few booths lined the walls around the small dance floor set up in front of the stage that took up the entire back wall. The bar was constructed of two logs split in half, sanded and layered with poly until they gleamed. Years of wear from elbows added character to it. A large mirror showcased the rows of liquor lining the shelves behind the bar. Classy, yet comfortable, was the feeling I had gone for and accomplished. The bar was much more sophisticated inside than out. From the brick fascia out front you would expect just another rundown dive bar, but I liked to surprise people.

Marla had her back to me counting the bottles that lined the wall, and making notations on her clipboard. She turned when I cleared my throat. She put her clipboard down. "Hey boss, what's up?"

"You got a minute? We need to talk."

"Not really, I need to get this inventory done before the evening rush." But she paused anyway and waited for me to go on. I sat on one of the stools strategically putting the bar between us.

"Well, it's time I made a few changes. I have a proposition for you."

She looked at me skeptically. "What sort of proposition do you have in mind?"

"I want you to manage The Silver Fox."

She laughed. "Don't I already do that?"

"In a way. I want it to be official though. Off the floor, out from behind the bar. I want you to take over the reins for me. This is an office position, with normal hours. I am going to be leaving for a while, and with the cubs I thought you might like having a day job rather than night shift."

"And who's going to take care of things at night?" she scoffed.

"I have some potential employees coming in. You will have final say, of course, but I think they all would work well. A bartender, bouncer, and two waitresses that could pick up the slack of losing you for the evening shifts. They are all new applicants to the pack that have been vetted and approved by the council, and Jerome."

"Are you saying I can't do my job and take care of the cubs?" She bristled.

I sighed. "No, that's not what I'm saying at all. You are the only one in the pack that I trust implicitly to run this show while I'm gone." I stood and went around the bar. "I don't know how long I'll be gone or if I'll be reachable all the time. I need to be able to go without worrying about the bar and what might happen here. You have been here the longest besides me, and I think it's time you have the title and pay you deserve. Plus, those cubs need a mom who's there when they wake up and when they go to bed. Suzanne and Jazz are wonderful, but don't you think it's time they have a mom that is more than a ghost walking by as they go to and from their lessons?"

I hoped bringing the cubs into play would deflate her anger and I was right. "Yeah. I hate when you do that. But not just anyone can come in and take care of the Fox. Who do you have coming?" She asked as a knock sounded on the door.

"Join me and find out."

Barrett, Janice, Allie, and David were waiting as I opened the door. I motioned them inside and locked the door. "Thank you for coming. This is Marla, my bar manager, and the person you will be working closely with. Have a seat and we can get started."

Marla growled low at me, not happy with being ambushed with employees she hadn't approved yet.

"I have read through your applications and know some of your backgrounds, but Marla hasn't had the same opportunity. If you could each give us the story on how you came here, why you applied, and how you would be an asset to the Silver Fox." I sat and motioned for Barrett to start. Marla sat next to me, clipboard in hand, and waited.

Barrett was a big man, lumbering over six feet tall, with the build of a wrestler. Dark brown hair in need of a cut curled around his ears. He had a scar along his left eyebrow adding a touch of danger to a face that welcomed trouble. He overflowed the chair he sat in. His jeans were well lived in and he wore work boots scuffed with age. He took off his leather jacket revealing a t-shirt barely containing the muscles beneath. Tattoos peeked from beneath his sleeves and ran down his arms. He was an intimidating man. His piercing gaze met ours. Eyes a dark chocolate brown rimmed with green as deep as a mossy forest floor.

"It's nice to finally meet you in person, Sterling. We have talked a few times, and you know most of my history, but, Ms. Marla, you need to know it all, too." He took a deep breath and leaned forward placing his elbows on his knees. "The last decade I have moved around a lot, my den was destroyed shortly after shifters came out. I fought beside my father as they murdered our family. When my father fell he made one last request of me—to save my brother at all costs. The decision to leave my father to certain death was the hardest I have ever had to make, but I took my brother and ran. Our mother had been murdered right before our eyes, and my sister had been captured. We tried to find her, but lost her scent after they drugged her and loaded her on a plane. We have searched for her ever since but have been unable to find where they took her. The loss drove my brother to insanity and he gave in to his animal side. He still roams the wild in Canada. I still hold out hope that I'll find her one day. Losing my brother put me into a dark place, and I knew it was better for everyone around me to be on my own. I skirted the edges of a few packs and prides watching and waiting to find the right one to join. If I had any hope of finding my sister, and the people who kidnapped her, I would need help. I spent five years in a cave high in the Rocky Mountains living off the land and laying low. Word of your pack made it my way and I thought it was worth checking out. One of the first to accept all species is known around the world, but when I heard about how you helped a female defeat one of the evilest Alphas out there, and then helped put her in charge. I knew you were my last hope." He took a deep breath as Marla scribbled on her clipboard.

"So, your main reason for wanting to join us is to gain access to our resources to help find your sister." Marla summed up.

"At first yes, but as I have talked with Sterling and Jerome my Bear has decided this pack could be more than a resource, that we might be able to find a new home here."

"I see, and if you have to wait for help? Weeks, months, even years? Would you be happy just working here and doing your part in the pack?'

I saw where Marla was steering Barrett, and it was a smart move. She was proving I was making the right choice in leaving her in charge. She put the integrity of the bar and pack as a priority, and expected nothing less of those working with and for her.

"Happy. I am not sure I know the meaning of that word anymore. I would say that I think I could be content to finally be useful to others again while I wait for the chance to search for my sister."

Marla motioned for him to continue his story as she made notes on her tablet.

"I am a Kodiak bear and grew up with my family in Alaska. I have picked up odd jobs here and there on my travels, always keeping my shifter nature a secret, never knowing who I could trust. With my size I either did manual labor, or more recently, I have been a bouncer at a few bars and clubs. When Sterling contacted me after I submitted my application and asked if I would be willing to work at the Silver Fox I said yes. I am not an Alpha by any means, but I'm strong, and I protect those that I trust." He looked at Marla. "I also protect females with all I am. I know how drunks can get and I won't put up with it. You can count on me to keep the peace here. I know I'll have to earn my place and prove myself, and I'm ready to do so. I'm tired of being on my own, I miss having a family and sleuth. If you give me a chance, I'll show you how much of an asset I can be." Barrett sat back and crossed his arms, waiting for a response.

Marla met his gaze. "Can you take orders from a woman, and a shifter lower on the food chain than you?"

Barrett smiled. "Yes ma'am. That's no problem. We Bears don't work on a "chain" of command, we work together as a team. You, ma'am, are the team leader."

She nodded. "Good, you start tonight. Now who's next?" She gazed at the three others sitting at the table. The sisters glanced at each other.

"We'll go," Janice offered. Both girls were average in height, no taller than five foot eight. Janice had light brown hair and Allie had hair black as ebony. They were complete opposites. Janice was petite and had a tomboy look about her, and Allie was curvy with a little extra weight in just the right places. Their eyes were the only thing the same. Both a deep amber color and full of life. Janice wore faded jeans and a simple tank top with no nonsense tennis shoes. Allie wore designer jeans, ripped for fashion rather than from use, and a flowy print top that accented her ample breasts but hid the extra padding along her waist. She finished off the look with a pair of heeled boots. The bar patrons would be attracted to both in their way.

"My name is Janice, and this is my sister Allie. We come as a set. We have worked as waitresses for the last ten years and know how to handle any kind of patron with ease and grace. Our clowder was small, just my parents, grandparents, and siblings. We always kept to ourselves, but when the local pack started growing we were given two options. Join them or go rogue. Everyone but my sister and I decided to join them, they didn't see any other option for survival, but Allie and I didn't like the Alpha, or his beta. They gave off an evil aura and we didn't want to be anywhere near them. Our cats hissed and scratched inside, and I knew if we stayed we probably wouldn't live long. In making that decision our access to our family was cut off. They were never allowed to see or speak to us again. We have stuck together since. It's easy to hide our animal sides among the humans, and working in bars helped. Even if we smelled funny to someone, we could attest that to the bar we worked in. Using heavily scented lotions, body wash, and shampoo helped, too. When we encountered another shifter, filtering through all of those scents is more of a hassle than many wanted to deal with."

Marla looked up. "How did you deal with the scents yourselves?"

"It was hard at first." Janice smiled. "She always wanted fancy perfumes."

"And she wanted to smell like a field of lavender," Allie shot back.

"We finally agreed to one scent that bridged both," Janice finished.

"It took about a year before our eyes stopped watering, and now we don't even notice it. We've become immune in a way, able to filter it out of the scents around us immediately," Allie offered.

Marla sniffed. "You smell normal to me. Cats, female, and a bit nervous."

"We chose not to bathe with scents today. It being an interview in a shifter bar, we didn't want to offend anyone's nasal passages." Janice and Allie laughed together.

Marla nodded in agreement and scribbled

more notes. "Continue."

"After ten years of moving we are both tired and ready to settle with a pack. Like Barrett, we heard about your pack through the grapevine and decided to check it out. We liked what we found so we applied. We didn't think it would take this long to get accepted, but we both realize that the council is thorough, and if it took a year for us to be accepted than anyone else in the pack went through the same thing and we should be safe. But like I said, we come as a package deal, we work together, live together, and protect each other."

Allie spoke up. "What my sister forgot to share is that we are bobcats. We are good at our jobs, and quick learners. We have no problem taking direction, and having a female boss is ideal for us." She smiled as she grasped her sister's hand.

Marla scribbled again. "Ok, but I don't need two waitresses on duty at the same time. Are you girls comfortable working opposite shifts on your own?"

"Yes," they said in unison.

"Good, Janice, I would prefer you for the day shift, and Allie, I think you would fit better on nights."

The girls looked at each other with knowing

smiles. "Yes, ma'am."

"Ok, that leaves you." Marla pointedly looked at David.

David fidgeted in his seat under her scrutiny. He was average to look at. Barely taller than the sisters, and much smaller in stature then Barrett, or even Sterling. The defining characteristic for David was his hair. Dark underneath with a crown of deep red brown. He kept it cropped close to his head along the sides and a bit longer on top, just enough to style back, but the redness glowed in the lights.

Marla took a deep breath. "What's your story? There can be no secrets if you are going to work here, and if you plan to make the pack your home Jerome won't have anyone who could be a threat here. I can't define what species you are. You're not feline, wolf, or bear. I haven't scented your kind before. So if you want the safety we offer, spill it." Marla didn't pull any punches. She gave it to you straight.

David sighed and mumbled, "I'm a crowned eagle."

Marla exchanged a look with me, puzzlement on her face. I already knew this, but wanted to see how David would explain himself. "Marla has never heard of the crowned eagle, David, can you explain?"

"I am one of only four known crowned eagle shifters left in the world. I grew up in Africa, our native land, until we were forced to move by the council. We were a quiet group. Our convocation, or pack, took care of each other and didn't want to get into shifter politics. We were doing fine until one of the local tribes saw my mom shift. At first we were accepted, they saw her as a Goddess. They started praying to her, asking for help we, of course, couldn't provide, and when a drought hit and they saw that no amount of praying changed that they blamed us and decided to hunt us down. We flew, but their arrows took my mom, brother, and most of our family. My dad and I made it out, and we hid in the mountains of Sweden." He wrung his hands as he spoke. Sharing his story with us was stressful, his body language and the sweat beading on his forehead were a dead giveaway.

"And where's your dad now?" Marla gently asked.

He looked up, making eye contact with Marla. "The cold took my father. He was old and past his time, he held on for me as long as he could. I gave him the burial he deserved and then took off on my own. In my grief I didn't pay attention, and while in my bird form I was caught by trappers. They caged me and transported me to the states to be sold to the highest bidder."

The girls gasped in shock next to him. He cringed but continued with his story.

"A collector of shifters recognized what I was and purchased me. He collared me, forced me to be a party favor behind his bar. I don't have the brute strength that Barrett has, or the cunning slyness to devise a plan that Sterling has, so for self-preservation I played my part for years. Ten years to be exact, until my owner died and his estranged daughter came to release us all. I wasn't the only trophy he kept. It was she who told me about this pack, and that I could find safety here. She gave me the application and enough money to get here."

Marla simply looked at him making David squirm in his seat. David looked at the others sitting with him. "I haven't had to wait as long as the rest of us, I don't know why, but I am thankful for that. I don't know if I would have made it on my own for long."

I spoke up. "Yes, David, your case was special. Jerome and I both saw that, and when we confirmed your story with the woman who helped you we decided to fast track your application. We offer you peace and safety, and when you are ready Jerome would like to speak to you about how you can eventually help the pack. For now I offer you a job, and Jerome offers you a place to stay where you don't have to watch your back every night."

Barrett spoke up. "No one will bother you while I'm here. We all deserve to live, and anyone who threatens that will have to deal with me."

I could already tell that this group would watch out for each other, and in time I knew that need to protect would grow to include the pack as well. I turned to Marla. "So, what do you think?"

She sat back. "I think they will all fit in fine. Allie, Barrett, and David, meet back here at four. Janice, I'll need you here at six am for the breakfast rush. We don't serve alcohol in the mornings, but we have a good rush of shifters that like to start the day with us."

I couldn't help but smile.

"Good, I have no more questions. Sterling has your paperwork so I will see you later." She stood and dismissed them as she made her way back to the office.

"I know this has been a whirlwind interview, thank you for coming so quickly. I look forward to getting to know you all better." I walked them out and thanked them for coming. I joined Marla after locking the door behind them. I found her behind my desk so I sat on the couch opposite her and waited.

"You know I don't like being ambushed that way, but I admit you chose well. When will you be leaving?"

"Not for a month at least. I want to make sure everyone is trained and you are comfortable with leaving the bar in their hands at night. I also want to make sure you get moved out of the apartment. I think moving David upstairs is the best option. The girls have a place, and Barrett will be staying with Jerome. David is staying at the house as well, but being around so many predators that could eat him for a snack will be uncomfortable."

"Move me where?!" she screeched.

"Jerome and Suzanne would like to talk to you about your options with the cubs. Tomorrow, while we are closed, go have lunch with them."

"That's when I planned to start training Janice."

"She can wait another day." I stood and stretched. "I'm going for a ride, I'll see you back here at four." I walked out waving at Jake as I went.

STERLING

I heard Marla mutter as I opened the back exit.

"Damn Alpha men, bossing me around. We'll see how well they like a pissed off cat."

I shook my head and laughed. For a feline who didn't like change, she was in for a ride.

CHAPTER 5

THE LAST TWO weeks had flown by in a whirlwind of training. I added Marla as an approved buyer on all the bar vendor accounts, and had just finished the paperwork at the bank to add her as an authorized signer so that bills would get paid on time. My phone rang as I walked out the bank door. "Sterling," I answered.

"Hey, we need to meet." Leo greeted me. He was a man of few words.

"OK, I just finished at the bank. When do you want to get together?" I glanced up and down the street checking for traffic before crossing. I wasn't going to be one of those idiots you see on YouTube videos that trip or get hit by a car because they are more focused on their phone than their surroundings.

"Meet me at the diner, I've already got us a table," Leo replied, and hung up.

The two blocks to Mo's diner took me five minutes to walk. The diner bordered the bad part of town but had the best pie in the city. The gumbo wasn't as good as the Fox's, but since I filched Jake from him that made perfect sense. Mo's looked like your typical old fashioned diner. Large windows, flashing neon sign on the roof hiding the second floor where Jake's old apartment was nestled, and metal exterior. Walking inside was like taking a trip back in time. Checkered tablecloths and a metal and Formica bar with pie displays dotting the surface. I found Leo in a back booth, facing the door. I made my way back and joined him. The waitress appeared with a fresh cup of coffee and menu.

"I don't need a menu, darlin', I'll just take a piece of chess pie please." I handed the menu back to her and she swished her hips as she walked away to get my order.

"You know they should just rename that sugar pie." Leo grunted.

"I know, but I still love that shit. Mo's is the only place in the city that serves it anymore."

"Yeah, because he doesn't care if it gives you diabetes or not. Every other restaurant has hopped on the health trend." Leo sipped his coffee. "Thanks for meeting me. I need you to leave a week earlier than expected."

"What's the rush?" I asked as the waitress placed my pie in front of me. I thanked her and she smiled, throwing me a hooded look that promised more than just sweet pie if I took her up on it. I blew her off and focused on Leo again. I didn't have time for any distractions with my upcoming travel. I took a bite, relishing the sweetness overload that hit my tongue and flowed down my throat as I waited for an explanation.

"I have had reports of increasing fights and vandalism. The Resistance is mobilizing, and I need you down there with Wyatt to handle it before the pack gets destroyed. The Texas Alpha is doing his best, but he doesn't have the experience or forces that we have. He has been trying to shift his pack and follow Jerome's blueprint but the local shifters have been uncooperative. That has allowed The Resistance to grow in members. They haven't done anymore than cause chaos so far, but we need to squash them before they do worse."

I leaned back, belly full. "If it's getting worse maybe we should take a couple more guys with us. Wyatt and I may not be enough to accomplish what you want." I had complete trust in Wyatt, but if The Resistance was growing we needed to take more force with us.

"I agree, so I already spoke to Jerome and Mack, they are sending help. Steven will join you and Wyatt when you depart, and Mack is sending Miguel to help as well. The four of you should be enough force to shut The Resistance down without it looking like we are trying to take control. I don't want to overtake the Texas pack, I just want to assist and support them until they are settled and thriving on their own. Plus, my potential investment in the bar is a corporate move that I want to see flourish."

"I see, so this move will benefit both you and Jerome. Adding another pack to Jerome's allies and lining your pocket with more cash. A win-win in both books."

"Exactly." Leo smiled, his predator evident in his eyes. "Can you do it?"

"Of course. I just have a couple more things to settle with Marla and then I'll be ready to go." I finished the last of my coffee. "Anything else?"

"No, that's all. The plane will be ready to take off Sunday night. Wyatt will be waiting for you."

I stood up, placing my napkin on the table. "I'll see him. If you need anything else before then you know how to contact me." I strode out the door and down the street toward my bike I had left parked in front of the bank. I dialed Jerome on the way simply stating, "Steven?" when he answered.

"I have been expecting your call, Sterling," Jerome replied. "Yes, Steven. His submissiveness will help you and you know it. Going in with too many strong shifters will hurt more than help. Steven can help show those lower in the pack that they have a place, too. You know that."

I knew he was right, but I was going into another Alpha's territory with little information. My fox was sly and smart, and high in the pack hierarchy, but that was known to only a few. I knew Wyatt and Miguel would be the brute force, I would be the brains, and Steven would be the comfort. Still, going against The Resistance with just the four of us made me nervous. "Should we contact Draven?"

"No, we have had no reports of Others in this uprising. I don't want to alert him if it's not necessary. If you find out information is incorrect and there are Others we will handle it as needed. Calling in Draven is a last resort. You and I both know that. Owing the vampire leader anymore favors is not in our best interest."

"Understood." I revved my bike and headed back to the Fox. I had four days to finish a few loose ends before I left.

CHAPTER 6

THE FLIGHT DOWN to Texas was uneventful. Steven and Wyatt rode with me in Leo's Learjet. We landed at a private air strip outside of town and were greeted by a hired car. Miguel had arrived a little earlier on a commercial flight. No one else in the pack knew of our arrival or why we were there. Wyatt and I had decided to come in under the pretense of a guy's weekend. The Alpha had agreed and gone through the normal process of approving our visit.

The driver of the car was a shifter, a coyote by his scent. Miguel was with the car when we disembarked the plane. He shook our hands addressing me when he spoke. "I've heard a lot about you. Mack has great respect for you, I am at your service."

"Thank you. I'm not sure what we are getting into here, so having an extra set of eyes to watch our back is welcome." I took a breath to talk to the driver holding open the back door for us. Miguel spoke before I could.

"It's no use, he won't chat with you. I've tried holding a conversation with him, but no response. I think the Alpha instructed him to be mute." Miguel looked sideways at the driver as we slid into the car, waiting for a response. "See, I can't even rile him up to communicate."

Wyatt opened his mouth to join the conversation. I caught his eyes and shook my head. I didn't want to discuss any of our business around ears I didn't trust. "I'm looking forward to a weekend without responsibility." I sighed and leaned back in the seat. Miguel took the hint and joined the conversation.

"Me too, I hear the fishing and hunting is vastly different here in the states than it is in Rio. According to the itinerary we will have plenty of both." He pulled out a manila envelope and handed it to me.

"I'm hoping to do a little hunting of the two legged female variety as well." Wyatt chuckled and elbowed Steven in the ribs.

"You guys enjoy yourselves. I'm here to make sure you have a sober driver, and to make sure you get back to the airport on time. No fun for me this trip." Steven crossed his arms and pouted, playing his part well. "Maybe next time I'll get to have the fun while someone else babysits."

"Don't feel bad, kiddo, you do well on this trip and I'll put in a good word with Jerome for you," I assured him. "You'll be taking your own guys' weekend soon. Patience, young padawan." We all laughed at the reference continuing with the ruse we had developed. The drive to the cabin was short. We were staying in guest housing on pack lands. The driver dropped us and our luggage off and left without a word.

I opened the pack link with Steven. *"Check the house for bugs and cameras."* He nodded in response as I spoke out loud. "I hope they stocked the place. I would hate to find the fridge empty; a beer sounds good after our flight."

Wyatt and Miguel grunted in agreement as we went inside. Steven took our bags to the bedrooms, scanning the cabin for any surveillance equipment while Wyatt grabbed beers from the fridge for us. Steven joined us in the living room, opening his hand to reveal three bugs and one camera. He then crushed them in his hand before speaking out loud.

"That's all I found, one in each of the bedrooms, and the camera was in the master bedroom. The rest of the house is clean. We can be free with our discussions now."

"Good work, Steven. Ok, now here are my thoughts." I sat forward and outlined the next two days. I wanted to head to the bar the following night, but during the day we had a fishing trip scheduled that we would stick to. We had to be vigilant with our cover, and act like shifters happy to get away from our packs and prides. "We need to pepper our discussions with a little bit of unhappiness at having to live with shifters below us in the food chain. How we don't mind being friends with other species, but being forced to live with them is altogether different. Wyatt, I think you and Miguel need to take the lead. They will never believe a fox such as myself is as high up in the hierarchy as I am."

"Sounds like a plan. We have to be quick about what we discover, and how we plan to take down this Resistance. The Alpha will be meeting us at the lake tomorrow. We will take things from there," Wyatt added.

I looked out the front windows scanning our surroundings. There were no other buildings within sight. We had been put at the edge of the land with acres of nothing around us. The cabin wasn't fancy, but a decent size. Three bedrooms, two baths, eat-in kitchen, living room, and a large porch. Under different circumstances I could see using it as a getaway, but it put me on edge how exposed we were. The furniture was old, but well-built, and sturdy enough for any shifter. The freezer was stocked with shelves of meat, and anything else we might want. Dishes were in the cupboards, and the bathroom overflowed with fluffy towels. The dressers in the bedrooms were full of t-shirts and sweatpants of all sizes. Not that we would need to use them having brought our own luggage and necessities with us. With only three bedrooms, one of us would have to sleep on the couch. Steven volunteered. "We should probably have a guard awake at all times anyway, and I'll take the night shift. I don't require much sleep. You guys need to be alert and fully rested when you're with the pack members."

I had hesitated when Jerome assigned Steven to this mission, but I should have learned by now to trust his judgment. Submissive yes, but he was smart, and willing to sacrifice his comfort for the end goal. I agreed and we retired for the night, preparing for the weekend ahead. I hadn't met the Alpha, didn't even know his name yet as Leo had done all the communicating. I sent a text to Jerome, a coded message to let him know we were here safe and had a plan of action ready before I turned out the light for the night.

CHAPTER 7

MORNING CAME QUICKLY along with a heat that settles into your bones and radiates through your body no matter how cold you have the air conditioning. My fox was not happy that we were having to deal with it. He wanted to be home in the cool forest taking his morning run. I joined the others on the front porch, choosing a cold glass of ice water over a cup of coffee. "So what is our plan for today, Wyatt?" I turned to him. As Leo's right hand man I was depending on him for the information we hadn't yet acquired.

"Plans have changed a bit. We have been invited to a brunch with the Alpha at the bar that Leo wants you to whip into shape. After that, he has graciously offered to have his top men take us on a tour of the pack land, and he has set up a hunt this evening. Mostly he is puffing his chest trying to show us how big and bad he is, but underneath he's scared. Leo has made it perfectly clear he won't put up with any crap, and if we find anything out of the ordinary we are to handle it and report back to him." Wyatt sipped his coffee. "Now is the time to relax, because we won't again until we are through with this and back home."

Miguel nodded. "I'm ready to do what it takes to straighten out this pack and get back to my pride."

A black Range Rover kicked up a dust trail as it sped down the dirt road to the cabin. I assumed it was our ride to the brunch as no one else should know we were out here. The windows were tinted so dark we couldn't identify who was inside. A quick sniff of the air as the driver's side door opened assured me there was only one person in the vehicle. The driver. He was a wolf, and he needed a shower, he stank of week-old beer and stale smoke. This wasn't a good sign, if he smelled that bad from yards away the bar must be horrible. Miguel descended the steps.

"You must be our ride to brunch."

"Yes," was the driver's reply. Nothing more. He stood by the car waiting for us. No small talk, no smile. I didn't know how his clothes weren't already drenched in sweat. He wore a long sleeved black button down shirt tucked into Levi's. Cowboy boots and dark sunglasses finished off his look. His hair was military short and blonde, the only light color on his body. He stood with his hands loosely held in front of him, his feet shoulder width apart. He looked confident, but he smelled of fear and something else. He smelled of sickness. I looked at Wyatt and quirked an eyebrow asking without words if he smelled the same thing. I lifted my nose slightly and inhaled, hoping he and Miguel took the hint. Wyatt's nostrils flared, and his eyes flashed when he caught the same whiff I did.

"Give us a moment to put our mugs in the kitchen and we will be ready." I addressed the driver and turned, knowing the other two would follow me. I turned the faucet on when we got in the kitchen. It wouldn't drown out our words but it would muffle them so he couldn't understand what we said. "Have you smelled that before?"

"I have smelled sickness, but not that. I don't know what is wrong with him," Wyatt said.

"I have." Miguel sighed. "My previous Alpha had the same scent, but he never admitted to being ill, or what was wrong with him. It progressed over the years, and made him meaner and less cautious. It's not a good thing, and we need to find out how many in this pack are ill.'

"Agreed." I nodded. "For now let's go have brunch. If the Alpha is infected that changes everything, and we will need to regroup with Leo and Jerome before moving forward."

We piled into the truck with our driver who had yet to introduce himself and didn't seem inclined to do so. He drove as if he were on autopilot, a shell of a shifter with someone else pulling his puppet strings. We attempted to start a conversation with him but got no response so we gave up and sat back taking in the scenery as we drove.

We were jostled to and fro on the thirty minute ride before we hit the edge of the town and an old worn out warehouse came into sight. The only indication that what we gazed at was the club was a mural painted on the side of a full moon with a howling wolf inside it, the Celtic triquetra designed into the fur. The warehouse had been converted into the only openly shifter friendly business in the town. The outside looked dilapidated, like something you would expect to be condemned by the city. Our driver pulled around to the back of the building, into a garage opening that took us to a state of the art parking lot. We parked next to a guarded door. This guard in full Armani suit, sunglasses, and earpiece.

"Sunglasses, underground, really?" Miguel

scoffed.

We exited the Rover and I immediately knew that my assumption of the guard as a shifter was wrong. "Vampire" I growled. Now the sunglasses made sense. To humans the eyes were the only thing that gave a vampire away. Their irises were ringed with red, showing how close to the edge their bloodlust was, always hiding right below the surface of their faked humanity. I whipped my phone out and sent another message to Jerome. Draven would need to be called in after all. This was becoming more complicated than we had anticipated. Wyatt and I followed behind the vampire with Miguel covering our backs. We were all on high alert, not sure what we would find around the next corner. If this Alpha was working with vampires, then witches were not far behind, and not the good covens like we have back home. The hallway smelled like oily black magic and put my fox on edge. Wyatt's dragon was close to the surface too, and I glanced back to see Miguel's eyes had already turned to that of his cat. I stopped.

"Get control, guys, we can't go into this meeting half shifted already. That would mean certain death, and I would like to return home in one piece."

A few breaths later, our animals under control, we continued on. The vampire simply stood waiting, and then moved forward. I didn't like this guy. None of us did. We arrived at a large metal door. Our escort stepped to the side as it opened from the inside revealing a tall thin female. Her raven hair was piled on top of her head, and her eyes had a ring of orange around the iris. Her body was covered in a flowing peasant dress belted at the waist, and her hands were covered with leather gloves.

"The Alpha welcomes you. Please come in and have a seat." She greeted us with an evil smile and oil-coated voice. I took a deep breath and the aroma of magic made the hairs on my neck stand up. I walked through the doorway, my poker face in place. I would give nothing away to this woman, she oozed danger and evil. We had just found our witch.

Scanning the room I noticed a wall of windows looking down onto the levels below. The bar and dance floor were empty at this time of day, but people I assumed were employees bustled about. Another wall held eight monitors, each one showing a different view or angle of the building that couldn't be seen through the windows. The opposite wall simply had a door. There were two leather couches facing the windows, a low table placed in front of them, and then to our right was a large desk with two computer screens and piles of papers. Finally, to our left, was a small conference table.

"Make yourselves comfortable, the Alpha will be with you shortly." She left through the door on the wall. Steven and Miguel moved two chairs from the conference table, positioning them so their backs were against a wall keeping all angles under watchful eyes. Wyatt and I went to the windows to watch the flow of work below us.

"They look like ants working in their mounds," Wyatt commented. I grunted in response. "These must be one-way windows. No one seems to notice us standing here."

"Could be, or they are all just scared enough to know not to look up here. I would bet on that rather than one way. I have a feeling this Alpha would get off on that kind of power." I cut off the rest of my statement as I felt another shifter close by. I turned so my body faced the door in the wall that the witch had exited, relaxing my pose. Wyatt chose to sit on the end of the couch angling himself the same way just as the door opened and the Alpha walked through. I knew it was him by the power he radiated.

His appearance surprised me, he was short and rotund with greasy hair, and what the girls back home would call a porn star mustache. Not at all what I was expecting. As he walked over the smell of sickness made my nose tingle and brought a taste of metal to the back of my mouth. He stopped and stretched his hand in greeting. "You must be Sterling. Leo told me you would be arriving. You can call me Ricky, it's a pleasure to meet you." Confidence flowed off him.

This was not the image I was expecting from my talks with Leo. This shifter didn't seem in need of any help or support. Either Leo's intel was wrong, or there had been a drastic change in the past week.

I shook his hand as my fox growled inside. Neither one of us liked this shifter. He was a snake to the core, and fox loved to hunt snakes. "The pleasure is mine. Leo didn't give us a lot of info, just that he wanted me to take a look and see if I could help you in any way," I responded.

Ricky laughed. "I don't know that we need any help here. Things have changed a bit since Leo and I last spoke, and at this time I'm not looking for an investor anymore, but you are more than welcome to check things out. Then you can go home and let Leo know that all is good." There was more info in what he didn't say than what he did. His eyes never stopped moving, trying to keep all of us in his line of sight. A sheen of sweat broke out on his forehead, and I could smell the underlying fear he was trying to hide. That mixed with the heavy layer of magic conveyed more than his words.

"Be as that may, I have a job to do, and I am always thorough. I will take you up on your offer of taking a look around. Including the books, as Leo instructed. Let me introduce you to my team." I took a step back and indicated Wyatt. "This is Wyatt, he is my security expert, and one of Leo's right hand men. I'll be having him take a look at your security to make sure it's up to par for both humans as well as shifters. Over there to your left is Steven, he's my finance guru, and he'll take a look at your books to make sure everything is on the up and up. And finally, there's Miguel, he has joined us from an ally pride to check on the shifters and humans that you have working for you. Make sure they are being treated well, and that they are here of their own free will."

Ricky didn't flinch, I had to give him credit

for his ability to keep a straight face. The stench of fear did ratchet up at my last statement. "As I said, everything is in order, you'll find that, and then you can report back and let Leo know that we don't need him. We are prospering on our own very well." Beads of sweat gathered along his hairline. "There really is no need to go over the financials and such."

I turned to watch out the window, giving him my back, a snub in the worst way. Any other Alpha would have taken offense, and by the intake of breath I heard, Ricky did, too. "We will see. I'm a little suspicious as to how you turned things around so quickly, and why you seem to have partnered with vampires." I waited a beat. "So I'd like you to give me a tour as my guys get to work."

Steven stood as I turned back around. "I assume you take care of finances in here, if you'll just leave a list of usernames and passwords I'll have Steven get started." Steven lowered his head at my statement in submissive agreement.

"And I'll tag along with you and Sterling so you can show me where the security office is." Wyatt smiled letting his dragon shine in his eyes briefly.

Ricky hesitated, looking between Wyatt and

Steven, and then focused on Miguel. "And what else will you need?" he huffed.

"Nothing, man, I'm good. I'll find my own way around." Miguel stood, stretched, and walked through the door in the wall that the Alpha had come through. I waited while Ricky got Steven set. He huffed as he leaned over Steven entering passwords as if he had forgotten the right one. When Steven made no move to leave the desk Ricky finally "remembered" the correct one and opened the files for him.

"Ok, I think that's everything, if you guys will follow me we can get the tour started. Wyatt, the security office is just down this hallway, we'll drop you there on the way." He smiled, having collected himself and standing tall again. The confident demeanor back in place. I noticed he kept reaching into his pocket, every time he did his calm and confidence bolstered a bit. The smell of tainted magic increased. I assumed he had some type of talisman there that was triggered when he touched it. I made a mental note to contact Jerome and see if we had any coven members near that could come help figure out the magic influence here.

"I got ya covered," Steven called as we went through the door. I turned to him and he pointed to his head and smiled indicating I had actually shared that last thought through the bonds. *"It's alright, boss, the magic here is screwing with our protection walls, I can hear Wyatt's thoughts too, let him know that,"* Steven shared through the bonds. I nodded once at him letting him know I got it. If Steven could hear Wyatt then the magic was strong. Non-pack members shouldn't be able to be heard. I made motions for everyone to cut off communication through the bonds, if we could hear Wyatt then it would make sense that Ricky and his goons could hear us, too. I wasn't positive, but until I knew for certain we needed to play it safe.

When we got to the security office, I took a look around while Wyatt sat down and familiarized himself with the system. I leaned over looking at the screen, really just getting close enough to whisper, "Double your mental walls." Wyatt didn't react but I knew he would be extra careful. "Let me know if you find anything that raises a red flag, otherwise I'll check on you after I get done with the tour."

"Will do, boss," Wyatt replied. Ricky jerked as his statement hit that a fox was in charge of this group.

Ricky led me through the hallways, pointing out that they had different levels for the patrons of the bar. It was more of a club now that he had his clutches on it he told me with pride. His office was on the third floor of the club, with the security office and a couple of VIP suites that were equipped with their own bar and bartender, couches, and windows like his office that allowed them to watch the patrons below. There was also a raised stage with a pole in the corner. "For private dancing if the girls agree." He laughed.

"What if the girls don't agree?" I asked.

"Well then they don't have to, but they won't be requested again. Those private parties bring big tips. No touching is allowed, of course, and clothes stay on, it's just added eye candy, and an easy way for the girls to make money." He shrugged his shoulders. "They don't seem to mind."

We made our way to the second floor which had more rooms, but these were much smaller and only had a couch or two, a TV on the wall that broadcast the dance floor, or DJ stand, and one wall was fully mirrored ceiling to floor. Again, they seemed like rooms you would find in a sex club rather than a dance club. Each of these rooms had a guard, and every guard was a vampire. "This floor is for our special clients that need to escape from temptation."

"You mean, these are rooms that the vampires can take their donors, willing or unwilling, right?" I was getting angrier the further we went.

"No donor is ever unwilling, they have to sign a contract before they are allowed in, both human and vampire, agreeing to the terms of the nest here. We have a great relationship with them. I don't know why we as shifters haven't collaborated with the vamps before now. It's been great for us."

"Because we weren't made to interact. The temptation for vampires will eventually get to be too much. Don't you know that shifter blood is like Absinthe to them, irresistible, and stronger than normal human blood? It's like a drug, once they taste it they want nothing else." I shook my head at this shifter's stupidity, and HE was the Alpha. More like someone's puppet.

"That's an old wives' tale, we have had no issues with any of the vampires around here. Their Master keeps them in check, and it's been a wonderful relationship. As you saw when you came here we even employ some of them. They are a great addition to the security team. Now let's keep going, the best part is next."

We ascended to the main floor where there was the most action. "Here is our main floor, where most of the fun happens. We dug this section out under the warehouse. We are below ground closer to the natural ley lines in this area which heightens a shifter's senses, and even adds to a human's experience. It heightens their emotions as well. We worked with the local coven to ward the whole club against negative energy, unwelcome guests, and other stuff. No fights have broken out since we did that. It's been a very happy experience."

I started feeling woozy as we approached the bar, the magic so thick in this part of the club that I felt like it was physically pushing down on me. The closer I got to the bar the heavier it got. Ricky didn't seem effected by it, actually no one around me did. The waitresses bustled around getting the tables and booths ready for the evening. I made it to a bar stool and sat hoping that I still looked in control on the outside. My fox was whining under the strain and pressure inside my head.

Ricky looked at me. "Hey, are you ...."

His statement was interrupted by a loud pissed off female voice. "I KNOW I'm late, if your damn driver knew where he was going I would have been on TIME."

"If you'll excuse me a minute." Ricky took off toward the voice. My fox perked, too. That voice was like a balm to the pain. I followed Ricky to see who she was.

"Reana, this is the fourth time this month you have been late," Ricky addressed her. She had her back turned hanging up a ragged black wool coat. Red hair full of curl and bounce swished around her shoulders as she turned placing her hands on her hips. My heart stopped and my fox growled in appreciation. She was stunning, standing there, Obsidian eyes blazing, her short nose turned up a bit at the end, her mouth pulled into a thin line, and her chin raised in defiance. I followed the luscious line of her neck to the crisp white button down she was wearing accenting her chest heaving with anger, without showing too much cleavage. She had curves, I loved a woman with curves. The black skirt she wore showed off her waist and hips to perfection landing just below the knee. A pencil skirt I think they are called. Her calves were muscular yet defined and she wore sensible kitten heels.

Fox yipped in appreciation and growled *"Mine"*. I shook my head at him. *"Yes,"* he responded, he was a stubborn one, and if I admitted it, which I didn't, he was always right.

Dammit, we didn't have time for this.

CHAPTER 8

REANA

ANOTHER DAY, ANOTHER half dollar. I stood on the porch waiting for my ride to work. Like I do every day. I'm so ready to get out of this situation, but the way Ricky runs this pack and territory I don't see that ever happening. I'm stuck, thanks to my own naïve stupidity. So here I stand in this god-forsaken uniform, my ride late once again, but I'll be the one to take the fall for that. It's never their fault, always mine.

As I expected, shit hit the fan when Ricky found me walking in thirty minutes late. Sam had already ripped me a new one, and I had had enough. I yelled at him, actually raised my voice. I straightened my shoulders, held my head high, and turned to face Ricky after he admonished me about my lateness.

"I'm sorry, sir. If your driver would arrive on time so would I. Or if you would allow me to drive myself this wouldn't happen again." I held my breath as I raised my eyes, but rather than focus on Ricky's left shoulder like I normally did, I knew better than to meet his eyes, my gaze strayed to the tall drink of water standing behind him. My inner fox hopped at the sight of him. Yes, that little bitch hopped, shaking her hips as I took him in. He was tall and slender, but not skinny. His frame spoke of defined yet understated muscle. His hair was salt and pepper, eyes a deep blue, strong nose and chiseled chin. His lips called to me as he gave me a small private smile. He was wearing relaxed denim jeans, a flannel shirt rolled to his elbows and tucked into the waist of his jeans, he finished the look with scuffed biker boots.

Ricky snapped his fingers in my face. "Reana, are you with me? Did you hear what I said?"

Shit, I had totally zoned out. "I'm sorry sir, no." I tore my gaze from the man behind him and stared at the floor.

"This is your last warning. I've told you before why you can't drive yourself. It's for your safety and ours. I will have a word with your driver. Until we get this under control, you are to check in when you are ready, and when you get picked up."

He was treating me like a child again. I hated this job. "Whatever you say, sir."

"Good, now get to work. We open in an hour." Ricky turned to the man behind him. "I'm sorry about the interruption, Sterling, this isn't the norm for my people. Reana is an exception, I give her more leeway than others because of her circumstances. But my charity only goes so far."

"I'd like to learn more about her situation, Ricky. Understand how your pack runs, and how it meshes with the club." The man Ricky had addressed as Sterling replied. My knees went weak at the sound of his voice. The timber of it sending vibrations down my spine as my fox perked up and whined *"want him, he's ours."* I shook my head. *"Not if he's part of Ricky's group. We won't be owned like that."* She took a long sniff. *"Smell him, not part of Ricky, not from here. Ours."* I ignored her and went to work.

I pushed her to the back of my mind to focus on the tasks at hand. The routine helped keep me sane and allowed me to continue working on my plan to get away from this pack. It would be harder now that they had started working with the vampires and that evil witch bitch. Ricky didn't think we knew about her, but it's the only way he became Alpha. The previous one had become ill and Ricky pounced on the chance to challenge him while he was down. He is a rat to the core—greasy, slimy, and totally dependent on the magic this witch had brought with her. I only had my theories to go on, but I had learned a long time ago to trust my gut.

My gut told me this witch was dealing with deep, dark, black magic. Blood ritual magic which wasn't good. Now she had her clutches in Ricky and most of those higher up in the pack. The pack had gone from almost extinction to a thriving, prosperous, and unbeatable group. I wanted out, my fox wanted out, and with each day I continued to work that possibility got farther and farther away. The loss of Tammy was a constant reminder of how horrible the pack turned after Jacob's, the previous Alpha's, death. What had been a pack on the rise, giving safety to those who requested it, has turned into a pack of corrupt, power hungry shifters. Ricky and his goons will hurt anyone, steal, lie, and I suspect even murder to get what they want. They rule through brute force and fear. They play favorites to anyone who has money, and turn a blind eye to their illegal dealings, providing them a safe haven to do business in the back rooms. I learned after Tammy's death to follow the rules, keep my head down, and not question things. I stuck to that most of the time, but once in a while I spoke before I thought, and challenged authority. I have been lucky that Sam, our wonderful bartender, always seemed to be there to help me out of the jams I got myself into.

Sam cleared his throat and nodded behind me just before a voice hit my ears.

"Excuse me, miss."

I turned and pasted my waitress smile on. "Yes, sir how can I help you?"

"My name is Miguel, do you have a minute?"

"Well, I'm getting ready for opening, I'm really busy." I knew Ricky didn't like me talking to anyone during prep work.

Sam came up behind me. "He's ok, Rea, you can talk to him while you set up."

I nodded, I hated when he called me that. My mom and sister had been the only ones allowed to shorten my name to Rea.

Miguel smiled at Sam and then to me. "Great, Rea, is it? I'll just walk with you. I promise to stay out of your way, I just have a couple of questions." Sam looked at me once more and left us alone.

"It's Reana actually."

"Oh, sorry about that. Reana." Miguel waited till Sam went into the back. "I'm not here to hurt you or get you in trouble. I'm with Sterling, the guy walking around with Ricky. I'm actually from a pride in South America, here on the request of a friend from the Black Mountain Pack to check things out here."

"I don't know how I can help you, I'm just a waitress here."

"You're more than a waitress. You observe more than we could ever take in, you know the ins and outs of the pack, and from what I'm feeling you're not happy to be here. You don't have to acknowledge that, but if you are willing to help me figure out what's wrong here, just give me a smile."

My fox was pushing at me inside, telling me this was our chance. I had to tread carefully, I didn't know Miguel, and he could be leading me into a trap. "I'm just a waitress, I keep my mouth shut and my head down. I don't think I can help you."

"I understand, if you change your mind, here is my card and a number you can reach me at." He placed the card and a folded paper into my hand. I didn't look at it and just stuck it into the pocket of my cocktail apron.

"I doubt I will, but thanks."

Miguel leaned in to whisper, "If you need

help call, anytime. I know things aren't right here, and you are the first shifter that I've met that doesn't reek of magic. We want to help. If you don't trust me, then call Sterling, his number is on there, too."

I nodded and went on to the next waitress smiling and greeting her. I followed him, the first glimmer of hope finding its way into my chest. Maybe they could help me. I tucked that thought away for now, I had a job to do, and a night shift to get through, so I focused on the tasks at hand. The doors would be opening soon letting in all the shifters, vamps, groupies, and wannabes. The last two groups grew each day as word got out about the club.

I have been working here for just over two years, and each night the crowd seemed to get bigger and bigger. This place used to be just a rundown dump that shifters could escape to. A place of refuge where there was no judgment and secrets were kept. Once they opened the door to humans, whether they were vetted or not, it pushed a lot of the shifters that were still in the closet to find another place to congregate. There was an underground movement in the making to take Ricky out as Alpha. His theory was that we all needed to be out and show the humans that

WE were in charge. He didn't want to coexist, he wanted to rule. His ideas were always pushed aside or ridiculed before she came.

At first I didn't realize anything weird was going on. Ricky started challenging those above him in the pack, raising his rank. Something that happens quite often when a member decides he doesn't like where he is. It's part of our history, the strong succeed and the weak follow. Over a few months he had advanced his rank and seemed to be an asset to the pack, until one day he skipped about five levels and challenged the Alpha for control. That's when everything went to hell in a hand basket. It was obvious he had cheated, had found some type of enhancement to help him win. The Alpha at the time finally gave in and ceded the win to Ricky. That wasn't enough for Ricky, he chose to kill the Alpha anyway. That's when she emerged, taking Ricky's hand and raising it in a boxer type win hold.

Rules changed that day, any challengers that came against him found themselves injured, dead, or they disappeared for good. He hasn't had to fight to keep his Alpha status since and I know she is the reason. No one knows much about her, other than she came from South America. She is pure evil, and is pulling Ricky's strings like a puppet master.

Miguel and his team just may be what we need to get out from under their tyrannical reign, if they don't die first.

I looked around, ensuring my tables were ready for customers and carried my tray back to the bar to pick up the tube shots and their holders. The doors opened, and I pasted a smile on my face, holding my tray full of shots high as I started working the crowd. The hairs on my neck stood at attention, signaling someone was watching me. I glanced up to the second-floor balcony to find Sterling staring at me intently. I kept my smile in place as a blush warmed my neck and I had to force my feet to move. Just his gaze made me tingle in places I had thought dead long ago.

This was going to be a hard decision, one I would need a clear head for, and if he stayed around would prove difficult. I tore my eyes away and focused on the customers surrounding me, vying for the first shot of the night.

Regulars flowed in filling the tables and booths, grabbing shots from my tray and my fellow servers as fast as we could refill them. Cash wasn't exchanged for these, they were the house special and always free for the first hour after opening. Sam explained it to me my first night. "Drunk people spend more money."So it was good for business according to Sam.

All I know is it gave the guys the idea that we were part of the deal. Free shot and free grope. When Sam realized that he started placing more bouncers strategically around the room.

Now the girls and I roamed in pairs serving back to back. The guys were just as happy to get a peek at some cleavage as they were grabbing our asses.

"I'm out again, Rea, how about you?" Suzy yelled in my ear over the thump of the DJ's music.

"Yeah." I waved at Sam behind the bar raising my empty shot tray and pulled Suzy behind me to the left side of the bar. That's supposed to be the waitress only section, though most nights it's just as packed with customers as the rest of the bar. Tonight it was empty and I was relieved. A few minutes away from the crowd was a blessing.

"This is no time to dilly dally, Rea, you've got drinks to serve." Sam barked over the music as he shoved another tray full of shots my way. "Fifteen minutes till those suckers have to start paying for them."

"Fifteen minutes till I can start actually

earning tips," I mumbled.

I joined Suzy back at our station and the hairs on my neck raise right before a warm body pressed against me. I knew just from his scent who it was, and so did my fox. She wiggled her hips and raised her tail in invitation before I shoved her back into submission. I didn't have time for her hussy antics. "And how exactly do you plan to earn those tips, love?" Sterling purred in my ear.

"Like any normal waitress, batting my eyes, smiling, and flirting with the drunks who actually think they have a chance," I responded with a little more attitude than I meant.

"And if they take it too far?" He placed his hand on my hip. With the grace of years of practice I gently took his hand with mine, twisting it as I turned pinching the Hegre pressure point between my thumb and forefinger. All without spilling a drink on my tray.

"I simply show them why they need to remember the manners their mommas taught them." I smiled sweetly.

Sterling's face flashed with surprise before settling into that cocky side grin he liked to wear around me. "You surprise me, little Reana. That pleases me, and makes fox proud."

"Darlin, I could care less if I please you or your fox. Now I need to get back to my job." I gave him my back trying to control my heart rate. My inner fox was nipping mad that I had turned my back on the man she had decided was our mate. I didn't have time to deal with a mate right now, but I would consider Miguel's words about their offer to help me get out of this pack.

"Hey Reana, we need a full round here." One of my regulars flagged me down.

"The usual, Todd?"

"Yup, you got it, and keep it flowing tonight, I have big wigs to impress." He palmed a hundred-dollar bill in my hand. This night was starting off great tips-wise.

"Sure thing, sugar." I winked, and the rest of the night went as usual. I felt Sterling's gaze on me all night, keeping that tingle of awareness alive in parts that had been dormant for years. Dealing with customers alone was tiring, add in the level of hyper awareness Sterling created and I was overly exhausted by the end of the night.

"Hey, Sam, all cleaned up, can you let my driver know I'm ready to go?"

"No need, Rea, he's already waiting for you." He inclined his head toward the end of the bar. My normal driver wasn't there, but Miguel and Sterling were. I tilted my head and raised an eyebrow in question. "Boss already okayed it." Sam shrugged at me.

"I hope you don't mind having a substitute driver tonight, Miss Reana" Miguel smiled as I approached them. Sterling stood next to him, holding my coat open, offering his assistance to put it on.

"If the boss okayed it, I guess I don't have a choice." Sterling froze at my statement.

"You always have a choice. If you prefer the vampire take you home I will have it arranged," he commented as he settled my coat on my shoulders and brushed his hands down my arms as I faced him. "I never want you to think the choice isn't yours. When it concerns us," he indicated Miguel and the rest of his team that suddenly materialized behind him. "You will *always* have a choice. We will never force you to do anything unless it's for your safety."

A laugh behind him caught my attention. "Sorry, ma'am," the shifter lowered his eyes and continued to smile. He was one of the group I hadn't met yet.

"Reana, meet the rest of my team. You've

met Miguel already. The jovial one you just saw is Wyatt, and over there waiting by the door is Steven." He waved and I waved back. "If you are ready to go so are we."

I was so tired I was falling asleep standing there. "Yeah, I can hear my bed calling me now."

Sterling held out his arm, and against my better judgment I linked mine through. "Your carriage awaits, my lady." I told myself it was because I couldn't maneuver on my heels anymore, but in all honesty I wanted to touch him again.

I took the opportunity to observe Sterling out of the corner of my eye as we walked. He wasn't overly bulky like many of the shifters in my pack, but he did look solidly built. His button down shirt and jeans fit him snugly, showing the strength beneath the fabric. The warmth radiating from him made me feel safe and cared for. A new feeling to me.

We stopped at a large SUV parked right outside the club doors. Sterling released me and held the back door open while Wyatt climbed behind the steering wheel. Steven took the front passenger seat, and Miguel walked around and sat in the back behind Wyatt.

"You're all going?" I squeaked.

"It's the most efficient option," Wyatt explained. "Sam gave us your address, and it's on our route back to our lodging."

"Do you mind?" Sterling whispered.

I did, but I couldn't admit that. Being in a vehicle with so many predators made my fox a little uneasy. "No, that's fine." I climbed in the back and scooted to the middle allowing Sterling room as I tried to calm my fox.

CHAPTER 9

STERLING

R<small>EANA'S NERVES WERE</small> evident as we drove her home. I wanted to wrap my arm around her and tell her everything would be alright, but I held back. She wasn't ready for that, and even though fox had claimed she was our mate, I didn't really know how loyal she was to Ricky.

After the shit storm Rook just cleared up in South America I had to be overly cautious. I had a gut feeling that the witch running things here is the same one Mack and Rook have been searching for. I learned to trust my gut centuries ago, it has never steered me wrong.

Wyatt pulled up outside of a rundown apartment building. Glancing around I instantly didn't like what I saw. Trash littered the sidewalk and a homeless man slowly made his way out of the alley. Miguel opened his door and I growled. "Close it." I angled myself toward Reana as much as I could in the confined space of the back seat. "This is where you live?" Miguel quirked his eyebrow at me over her head. He had smelled it, too.

"Yes, it's safe enough. All the single waitresses live here. It's part of the "benefits package,""Reana answered, using her hands to put air quotes around the last two words. "It's not bad really. With the guards it's the safest building in the neighborhood."

"And you're okay with those guards?"

"The vamps." She shrugged. "Like I have a choice. They have left me alone, and I think there is some kind of spell on them. They can't touch any of the girls that live here." She took a deep breath. "I tried talking to them, and when I get close they recoil in pain. They have cleaned the neighborhood of drug dealers and the gangs, so it's safe enough."

My fox perked up, unhappy that she kept using the term 'safe enough'.

"Humph," Steven chimed in.

"Still, I'd feel better walking you to your door, if that's okay with you." This woman, who had been living a life with no choice of her own needed to know she would always have a choice with me. *"Not her choice. Must protect mate."*Fox wasn't happy I was giving her a choice. We weren't in the wild, and her hesitation confirmed she didn't trust us. Careful maneuvering would be needed around her. Fox didn't like it, but calmed and let me take the lead for now.

"I'm good, thanks," she replied.

"Please," I implored. "I don't think I could sleep well tonight if I didn't. My mam raised me to be a gentleman, and that means never letting a lady walk to her door unaccompanied." I gave her what I hoped was a megawatt smile.

Reana considered me for a moment. "Well I wouldn't want you to disappoint your mama." She gave me a coy smile.

This creature standing here confused the hell out of me, strong and stubborn one minute, and then flirty and shy the next. *Whew*. This time I was positive she had flirted with me. Fox and I were going to run with it. I nodded at Miguel who exited the SUV and scanned the surroundings. When he deemed it safe, he opened the door on my side, allowing me out, and I held my hand up to assist Reana. She took my hand after a moment's hesitation, and before she could let go I clasped it and threaded her arm through mine to escort her in. Taking full advantage of how close it brought her body to mine. Miguel opened the building doors for us, and then stood guard right outside them. I knew he had my back. The stairway inside wasn't very wide, two people would have to turn sideways to pass. The dilapidated elevator was even less encouraging. I knew from the address Sam the bartender gave us that Reana lived on the third floor. I took her hand from the crook of my arm and twined my fingers with hers as I stepped toward the stairs.

She pulled against me to stop. "The elevator works fine, it just looks like junk." She tried to take her hand back but I wouldn't relent.

"And your fox is okay with the confinement? Even for that short of a ride? Mine would prefer the stairs, three flights isn't a long climb." I pulled her to me, trapping her hand against my chest and looking into those big round eyes. Her irises were dilated and her nostrils flared with lust she fought to hide.

"How do you know what floor I live on?" she whispered, her voice a quiver of breath.

I just cocked my head and smiled. All the while tracing patterns on the back of her hand with my thumb until the pieces clicked into place and she realized where I got the information..

"Sam." She clenched my shirt without thought. "Damn him."

"Don't blame Sam, it was an order from Ricky." I smiled. "So, small, slow, climbing box of potential death or three flights of stairs?" Her gaze had dropped to my lips as I spoke, my tongue flipped out to moisten them as I spoke, making her breath hitch.

She shook her head as she looked between the elevator and stairs. "Stairs will be fine."

"Okay then, I just need you to release my shirt and we can get you home." I chuckled. She gasped relaxing her hand, trying to pull it away from my chest. I wouldn't let her, instead I turned her hand palm up and laced my fingers through hers and started up the stairs, keeping her close behind me. I pressed our linked hands against my lower back, keeping her no more than a few inches away from me. Her scent of arousal deepened with each step we took until I was sure she had to have soaked through her underwear and was dripping down her legs. The thought hardened me instantly. I had been keeping myself under control until that moment. I wanted to turn around, push her against the wall and raise her skirt to see if I was right. Images of her legs wrapped around me, head thrown back in passion revealing that creamy neck flashed through my head as my erection pressed harder into my zipper. The bite of metal against my most sensitive skin jarred me from my daydream. I looked up to see we were at her door. I let go of her hand and held mine open. "Keys?"

"What? I'm good. You escorted me to my door. You can go." She focused on searching through her bag expecting me to go. So when she looked up having triumphantly found her keys, I snagged them and opened her door.

"Stay here while I make sure it's clear." I didn't expect her to comply. Her scent had quickly gone from aroused to pissed off. My little mate was a spitfire I had a feeling.

"Wait, you want me to wait? This is MY apartment, and is the SAFEST in the neighborhood. You saw the vamps outside. NO ONE with half a brain would even think of breaking into ANY one of these apartments. Especially MINE." She stopped abruptly.

I turned slowly to face her. "What do you mean, "especially mine?""

"Nothing. Just... Thank you for walking me to my door. I'll take it from here." She tried to brush past and grab her keys which I quickly held out of reach.

"Please, to ease my conscience, let me

check first." I gave her what I hoped was my most endearing smile, pleading with my eyes.

She huffed and crossed her arms beneath her chest. Drawing my eyes down to those perfect globes just begging for my touch. "Fine."

I entered and scanned by scent before doing a walk through. Her apartment was small but efficient. A one bedroom with conjoined kitchen and living room, a bathroom and short hall separating the spaces. Her furniture was old but clearly well cared for. A loveseat and wingback chair flanked a coffee table made out of old pallets, but no TV. Just a bookshelf crammed full of a variety of books from Stephen King to steamy romance, and hidden in between I caught a name I recognized. I pulled the book out and I raised an eyebrow. "Jenna Jacob, you read her?" Her face darkened to a rosy pink as she stammered.

"A friend gave them to me. I haven't read them yet."

"You should, she is an amazing writer and very insightful into the lifestyle. If you are interested in that." I flipped through the book in hand.

"You've read them?" Her surprise showing in her raised eyebrows.

I looked straight into her eyes. "Yes, the

first was simply on a dare from a friend, but I got sucked in and downloaded the rest. She's a great storyteller, and she has a way with the sex scenes, they even made me blush, but I also learned some things from her writing." I closed the book still watching her. Her scent hit me followed by the sound of her heartbeat, fast and excited. That mixture spoke to me without words. I placed the book on the coffee table with purpose. It was time for me to leave. Holding fox back was becoming difficult with my focus so split. I didn't want to scare her or take her without her full consent. I adjusted myself hoping to alleviate the need building. "I should go. Everything seems secure, but feel free to call if that changes, you get scared, or just want to talk." I smiled.

Her voice stopped me at the door. "Thank you, Sterling."

I looked ahead, knowing if I looked at her I wouldn't be able to leave. "You're welcome, Reana." Adding in my own mind, *'anything for my mate.'* Her sharp intake of breath as I walked out made me wonder if she heard my thoughts. I had heard that mates, even before bonding, could catch snippets of each other's thoughts, but had never experienced it myself. I smiled.

I imagined her picking up her book to read tonight, and imagining me in the role of Master. Fox liked that idea as well. I was still grinning as I exited the building.

"What happened up there? You're grinning like a cat full of cream." Miguel chuckled. Steven lounged against the SUV. "Nah, man, that's his 'the chase has begun' grin."

I wiped the grin off my face. "Miguel, you ever compare me to a cat again I'll let fox out to play with your kitty." I glared at them all.

"And that is the 'shut the fuck and get back to work' glare," Wyatt added. "Now hop in, boys, Leo acquired better and more secure lodgings for us."

CHAPTER 10

REANA

I WATCHED STERLING LEAVE hoping I hadn't heard him correctly. *"Mate,"* rolled around in my head, my fox jumping in excitement. *"Yes, mate! Our mate found us."* I shook my head. "Look here, missy, I don't have time for this. I'm barely hanging on in this life as it is, a mate will simply screw it up. You know how Ricky feels about his "girls" finding their other half. I'd like to live a little longer, don't you?" *"Mate can handle Ricky."* Flashes of Ricky lying prone in a forest somewhere ran through my head. Exactly how my fox would love to see him. "Stop, he's a fox too, remember, he can't take on Ricky. He's an Alpha, with his witchy enhancements."

"Not alone, but he has friends. Good friends."

She had a point, but I didn't dwell on it. Letting in any hope only hurt worse when it was crushed. I went and turned the locks on the door and began my routine for bed. I hung my coat on the hook by the door, took my heels off, and placed them side by side on the floor beneath it. I put the kettle on for tea and stripped out of my uniform as I entered the bedroom. I sniffed it, checking to see if I could get one more night out if it before washing. The shirt was a lost cause, too many drinks spilled tonight, but the skirt could last another night. I hung it up, and put my blouse in the bag for the cleaners. I stood in my small closet standing in just my bra and underwear. I had two blouses left, and one skirt, so a week's worth of uniforms. I would have to send one of the guards to the cleaners for me tomorrow.

I scoured through the laundry basket by my bed where I kept the few comfy clothes I had and pulled out an oversized t-shirt nightgown. I slipped it over my head, and then removed my bra dragging it through the slack in one of the arms. The kettle whistled as I was hanging it after spraying it with liquid fabric softener. A trick a former coworker had shared with me. Hand wash it once a week, and spray it with fabric softener every night, let it hang, and it would last twice as long.

I set my steaming cup of tea on the coffee table as I settled down to relax a bit before bed and saw the book Sterling had found in my shelf earlier.

One of the waitresses had given it to me, thinking if I didn't have a sex life I could still at least have a good steamy read while I "serviced" myself. I had hidden it as soon as I got home and hadn't looked at it since. My curiosity was piqued knowing that Sterling read books like that, so I picked it up and flipped to the first page. My face was hot and dormant girlie parts were tingling by the fifth page. I put the book down and grabbed my mug, taking a healthy sip of tea trying to calm myself. I stared at the book imagining Sterling reading it, getting as excited as I did and how he would have dealt with it.

I finished my tea and put my mug in the sink. Turning out the lights the book called to me again. I grabbed it as I headed to bed. A few more pages I told myself. My little alarm clock read four am as I closed the book having finished the last page. I was too worked up to go to sleep now, so I reached over and pulled the single toy I owned out of my nightstand. I hadn't felt the need to use it in a long time, but imagining Sterling in the main character's role as I read had me so worked up I needed a good release. I knew it wouldn't take much, and sixty seconds after the vibrations hit my already engorged clit the orgasm overtook me, releasing pent up energy. Sterling's face in the front of my mind the whole time. I cleaned up, sanitized my toy, and turned the light off finally able to succumb to sleep.

"How the hell am I going to face him again?"

"Mate will know and love it," my fox said with excitement. "He wants us just as much."

"Well he can keep wanting, I don't have any room for a mate in my life right now. I have to focus on how to get out of this hell hole and away from Ricky, alive."

I fell asleep thinking about the last girl who had tried it, she had found her mate and wanted to settle down. Ricky had let her leave, but as she and her mate were leaving town they had been hit head on and both had died. The car had burst into flames, and even the fire chief couldn't explain it, the damage to the car did not correlate with an explosion. I knew the truth, but held it inside for my own protection. So now none of us even tried to leave for fear of death.

Two other waitresses had found their mates, but had refused them. The constant battle with their animal sides had driven one of them insane, and the other had transferred jobs so she worked in another pack-owned business where she answered phones in a basement all day, effectively keeping her mate away from her. I don't know if she was still there or not. Again rumor said she had taken her own life rather than deal with the pain of being away from her mate.

Both males were now part of Ricky's guard, and essentially robotic zombies. I am pretty sure the witch is keeping them that way. Proving that once you join the pack there was no way out.

My dreams that night bounced between scenes in a pleasure dungeon with Sterling in control, and scenes in a real dungeon being tortured by Ricky, a no faced woman at his side. I woke in a sweat the next afternoon exhausted, dreading my shift at work that night. I didn't have any food in the apartment, and having slept so late I didn't have time to run to the store. Going in early for dinner was my only option if I wanted to stay on my feet and not faint from food deprivation during my shift.

Even a fox shifter like myself needed to eat lots of calories on a regular basis due to our high metabolism. Many of the others in the pack thought since I was a small animal I didn't need as much, but the size of our animal didn't make a difference. I could eat just as much as the wolves that guarded

Ricky. I texted Sam to let him know I wanted to come in for pack meal tonight, and he replied that the driver was on the way.

My issues with this pack just kept getting worse. Having a driver was another. The women were not allowed to have vehicles or drive themselves anywhere. We were supposedly "sacred", and needed to be "cherished" and "taken care of."So we were all assigned a driver once the agreement with the local nest of vampires had been put into place. My driver was one of the first vamps to step up and help out. He was old, older than most in the area, and had a good handle on his bloodlust. Many of the younger ones had to be spelled. Like the ones guarding the apartment building. The spell wore off after time and had to be renewed, but my driver didn't need it. He was pleasant enough, and had informed me early on that shifter blood didn't agree with his palate. Or so he said in the single conversation we had when he was introduced as my driver.

Our rides were usually silent, but this evening was different. He was waiting when I left the building holding the back door open for me. As I passed he bowed. He never bows and it made me stop. "What was that for?" I didn't expect an answer, as he had never answered any of my questions before and had been driving me for the past year. As expected he didn't answer, just stared over my shoulder, or well, I think he did. I couldn't tell with the sunglasses he always wore. "I'm not getting in until you tell me why you just bowed." I crossed my arms and stuck my hip out for emphasis.

"It is required," he replied, standing stoically in the sun, still looking over my shoulder.

"Since when? Why? What has changed? Do you bow to all the women you drive around?"

He sighed heavily and took his sunglasses off, revealing his eyes to me for the first time. They were a brilliant green with a ring of red, and they seemed illuminated from within. His eyes met mine as he said, "When the Head Master of vampires tells you to do something you don't ask why. I do not have the answers you seek."

"Does Ricky know about this change?" I quickly thought to ask while he seemed in a mood to chat.

"I don't know, but orders from the Head Master supersede any your Alpha may give us. Now please get in, the sun is rather warm."

"Will you continue to talk to me if I do?" I threw back at him.

Again a great sigh escaped his lips. "If that will get you in the vehicle, than yes. Though I warn you, I do not have the answers you seek."

I nodded my head in satisfaction and climbed in the back of the SUV. He closed the door behind me scanning the surroundings before he got behind the steering wheel. As soon as he had put the truck in drive I started with my questions.

"What is your name?'

"Alexei, but you may call me Alex."

"OK, Alex, how did you become my driver?"

"I was assigned the job."

"By Ricky?"

"No, by my master."

"I thought Ricky was in charge of you guys." The little bit I was getting from Alex was enlightening.

"We agreed to an accord, but he is not in charge of us, and neither is his witch."

"So you guys aren't under her spell?"

"We are here."

I looked out the window to see we were at the back door of the warehouse. I climbed out when he opened the door and headed toward the entrance. I realized I didn't hear the SUV drive off like normal and the guard at the door bowed as I approached.

I turned and almost ran into Alex. "What the hell, Alex? Are all the vamps going to bow to me?"

"Most likely. When the head of all vampires gives an order it's followed. When Sterling claimed you Draven's protection came with that claiming," he replied in his deadpan manner.

"That's not going to work, others will talk, and it makes me a big target. Plus, if Ricky doesn't know about it he's going to flip out. You guys don't even bow for him," I huffed.

"You have a point." He stood silent for a moment, still as a statue. "It's been taken care of. No more bowing."

I could have sworn a small smile teased his lips, but it was gone so quickly it could have been my imagination.

"Good." I gave him my back and strode through the door the guard was holding open as I heard the engine of the SUV come to life signaling that Alex was leaving. I let out a breath I didn't realize I was holding and navigated the hallways until I reached the small dining room that the employee meals were served in.

Many of us had odd shifts and the club was in the basement which made it hard to tell whether it was morning, afternoon, or night. Sam had decided, after much debate with Ricky, that meals would be provided for any employee currently on duty or getting ready to start. I rarely ate with the others since I had an apartment away from the club, but with oversleeping I didn't have a choice.

I draped my coat over a chair and grabbed a plate to fill at the table of food laid out.

"Hey Rea, what are you doing here? You never eat with the rest of us." Suzy approached me holding her own empty plate.

"I woke up late and have no food in my apartment, so I decided it was eat here or faint from hunger later tonight. I didn't want to twist an ankle, so eating with all you slobs was my only choice." I grinned and winked at her, letting her know I was playing.

"I see how you are, Miss High and Mighty, too good to eat with us poor peasants, eh?" She laughed at me.

"You ready for tonight?" I asked her.

"Didn't you hear?" she gasped. "Tonight the club has been closed to the public, it's being rented out for some big private event. They even requested special uniforms, I have yours in the locker room."

"What, since when?" Her statement made me falter a bit in my steps. Plus, the thought of requested costumes sent a shiver down my spine.

"Oh, it can't be that bad, the costumes don't show anything. Long tailored pants, tank top, and jacket. Very classy, and the shoes are half the heel height we normally wear. I think you'll like it. The only other request was that we wear our hair up off our necks."

Her last words made me stop and face her fully. "You know what that means, don't you, Suzy?"

"No, what?" she replied in her ditzy innocence.

I grabbed her arm making her look me in the eye. "This special party, is a party of vamps. If they have the money to rent this whole place they probably aren't on Ricky's payroll." When it finally clicked in her head her eyes got bigger than the tea saucers sitting on the tables. I patted her arm. "Stay close to me tonight."

I didn't know why I felt that would help, but after the way I had just been treated by Alex and the guard upstairs I felt that I might just have a bit of sway with the vamps, if they were from the local nest, and could maybe keep Suzy safe at least.

Dinner didn't seem so appetizing anymore, but I sat and ate anyway knowing I'd need the strength for whatever was to come. My fox was impatiently pacing while I stressed over tonight's predicament. *"Mate will protect us."* That was always her answer, though I was beginning to believe her. I still thought having a mate would sign my death certificate, but maybe being with Sterling would be the best way to die. Or maybe he might be able to protect me from Ricky. He seemed to have some dangerous friends. I couldn't deny the attraction I felt for him, or how safe I felt next to him. We did have that 'talk in our heads' ability as well which could come in handy, and according to Sterling is a sign that we are destined to be mates.

I decided then to talk to Sterling some more about it. We still didn't know much about each other, but the way the stories go is that you just know when you have found your mate. The Fates choose for you, getting to know them happens after the mating frenzy subsides. Each mate is chosen to balance another. A dream all shifters have. A dream I never thought could come true for me.

I looked around the table at my co-workers and pushed the food around on my plate while they ate. Every one of them was content, and seemingly happy all the time. They all thought Ricky was fabulous and the changes he had made to the club were for the better. Well, all of them except Sam, he felt the same way I did, that something wasn't right and the witch was behind it. There was nothing the two of us could do to change it, so we kept our heads down and followed the rules simply to save our own skin.

Now though with a private party closing the club, the special treatment my driver had given me and the arrival of Sterling and his team that may just change. At least I hoped it would.

CHAPTER 11

STERLING

"**S**O WHERE ARE we headed, man?" Miguel asked.

"I think he got us digs at the corporate suites," Wyatt replied.

"Oh, fancy," Miguel teased.

Steven and I sat in the back in our own self-contemplation. Fox was not happy that we were leaving our decided mate.

"She'll be ok, she is surrounded by protection that won't hurt her." Steven spoke through the pack bonds.

"I know logically you are right, but emotionally I want to rip the door off and run back to her, even if I only get to guard her door."

"They tell us that's what happens when you find a mate. An uncontrollable need to see, touch, protect them all the time. The further away you are, the more intense the feeling," Steven replied, keeping our conversation through the bond rather than vocally. "If you allow me to touch you briefly

I may be able to ease the ache."

I nodded my consent, willing to try anything to ease this restless need to get back to Reana. Steven placed his hand on my bicep, closed his eyes and breathed deeply. A few moments later, to my surprise, the need inside faded from a roaring demand to a slight whimper in the back of my mind. I was shocked that a simple touch could help that much. Steven let go and slumped a little in the seat next to me.

"Wow, thank you. I've never experienced that before. Are you ok?" I continued the conversation through the pack bond so as to not draw attention from the front seats. I was curious to his talent, and the benefit it could bring to the pack, as well as possible future needs on this particular mission.

"Some submissives have the gift, though from my discussion with Jerome I am the only one in our pack. We keep it secret because it takes a lot out of me, and if I use it too much it could drain me to the point I may not recover. I am here whenever you need, Sterling, but can we keep this between us for now?"

I nodded in agreement and turned my attention to the conversation happening in the front seat. Thoughts of Reana were still running through my mind, but the need to rip the truck door off and run back to her was now under control.

"So where do you think we need to go from here?" Miguel directed his question to me. "We all know that things aren't right here, and black magic swirls around almost everyone."

"I'm not sure, a conference call needs to happen when we get to the apartment between Jerome, Leo, Mack, and Draven. We have more elements at work here than just a rise of The Resistance. For now we wait, refuel, and try to rest."

Wyatt entered a parking garage and drove down instead of up, entering a passcode into a keypad which opened an elaborate gate before us. He parked and we got out to follow him, another code entered at the elevator, and a third once we were inside. The elevator slowly chugged upward, spitting us out on the top floor right into a penthouse apartment, fully furnished, with views of the city below. Miguel whistled as we exited and made our way into the main living area.

"This is one of Leo's secure locations when he travels," Wyatt informed us. "We have no need to monitor ourselves as the codes are changed weekly and sweeps are made daily for listening devices and cameras. Leo had the kitchen stocked earlier, and our bags should already be here. His staff is most efficient," Wyatt shared as he grabbed us beers from the fridge. "What's the plan, Sterling? I know we call the higher ups tomorrow, but your brain is always chugging four steps ahead."

I finished the pull from my beer and nodded. "Right you are. Removing this cloud of magic is going to be difficult. But that's first priority. We will leave the vampires to Draven with the agreement that any who attack us will be destroyed. I don't have time to capture and babysit those blood suckers. We need to find someone willing to side with us, someone who knows all the ins and outs of what Ricky is doing."

"I think I can help with that," Miguel interjected. "I made a few friends this evening, and not everyone in his inner circle is brainwashed yet. Let me work on them a bit more tomorrow. I have a fella's number. I'll give him a call tomorrow and see if he's willing to meet outside the club."

"Good, we'll run that by everyone in the conference call tomorrow." I relaxed back onto the couch, still fighting the feeling I needed to get back to Reana, and tried to keep my focus on the discussion at hand. "What did you discover in your perusal of the financials?"

"Everything was clean. Too clean. No business has that perfect of records with continued growth in income," Steven reported. "The files he gave me access to have to be false, I can't prove it yet, but I know they are. There is no reason for the owner to have contacted Leo for help if those files are correct. I did find one encrypted file, but didn't have time to examine it. I don't know if I could break the code or not, but I'm sure Leo knows someone who can. I sent it to my phone so we can ask tomorrow and I'll send it on."

"Miguel, how about the morale of the workers, and pack members?" I tilted my beer back finishing it off.

"They seem to be one happy family, all in love with Ricky and his sidekicks. Except for Reana and one other waitress who I think have avoided drinking the "everyone loves Ricky" party punch. The vamps didn't even have a bad word about him. The patrons love the club and what it's changed into. It's all too Brady Bunch happy for me," Miguel quipped.

At the sound of her name my mind wandered back to how it felt having her hand in mine as I walked her up the stairs. The hand of a hard working woman, calluses on her palms from waitressing, contrasted with the soft suppleness that I encountered when I rubbed my thumb across the back of her hand. Showing that she took care of her skin and giving me a glimpse of what the rest of her might feel like. Fox and I loved the anticipation that began to build for the next time we would see her. We needed a few hours of sleep though. "Okay, I think that's all we can do for now, we need to catch a few hours' sleep. Meet back here at 0800 to make the call. Time is of the essence, and the longer we are here, the more likely our true purpose will be discovered."

Steven gathered our bottles and put them in the recycling bin as we dispersed into the bedrooms. None of us would get good sleep, but rest was needed to function at our highest. We couldn't do much else tonight anyway, we needed back-up and guidance from the Alphas and their seconds. So we would wait till morning. I stripped and plopped on the king size bed in my room. Throwing my arm over my eyes as I lay on my back and let my mind to wander to Reana, and what fox and I would do to her when we got her in our bed. My lips tilted slightly at the thought, a wicked smile beginning, we couldn't wait. Though the chase would be hard, I knew Reana would be worth it in the end.

The smell of fresh coffee and frying bacon drew me out of my sleep the next morning. I could hear the muffled voices of Steven and Wyatt through the bedroom door. I dressed and followed my nose, nodding at Miguel as he exited his room at the same time. We both made a beeline for the coffeepot.

"Jet lag is the worst on the third day," Miguel grumbled. "Adjusting to time change sucks."

"Now that you both have joined the land of the living I can stop wasting my time listening to this one jabber on about nothing," Wyatt announced with a laugh. The look on Steven's face was priceless. I had never known that man to jabber about anything. "Leo should be calling any moment to conference us in. I talked to him early this morning before the sun came up and gave him the report so far. He said he would call when he had Jerome, Casey, and Draven on the line."

"Casey? I thought we would bring Mack in on this," I replied.

"Nope, Casey is Alpha, and any help or assistance has to go through her, you know that. Leo treats her no differently than any other Alpha he works with. I did let him know that we would like to request Rook's assistance, so we will see how that goes."

I took my coffee out onto the balcony and watched the city below awaken as the sun rose over the buildings. Everything was so much louder here, and the stench of exhaust from all the vehicles zooming about assaulted my sinuses. I immediately returned inside and shut the sliding glass door blocking out the sound and scent. I grabbed a couple strips of bacon to munch on as I read the paper that had been left on the counter. Steven silently joined me.

"How are you feeling this morning? Do you need my assistance again?" Steven inquired through the pack bond.

I replied, "No, it's bearable this morning, I appreciate the offer. I'll let you know if it gets to be too much. Thank you, Steven, you and your gift are a blessing to have on this mission with us. More than you'll ever know." He nodded at me and left me to my reading.

Reana had been a constant thought in my mind since that first glance. The anticipation of seeing her tonight quickened the beat of my heart and fox hopped around inside in excitement.

We both were acting like kids on Christmas Eve, anticipating the unwrapping of gifts meant only for us. I know that's how peeling her clothing off will feel and I plan to savor every moment when I do. Fox yipped in agreement.

The phone rang and was immediately answered by the sound system in the apartment. Leo's voice boomed at us from every speaker in the room. "Good morning, gentlemen, are we ready for this?"

"Let me turn the volume down on you and we will be," Wyatt yelled.

"You don't need to yell, the speakers in the room have microphones that will pick up a flea's sneeze. Normal voices are satisfactory. Hold a moment and I'll connect us all."

We all sat in the living room as we awaited the final connection. This should prove be interesting, conference calls usually ended in a chaos of shit because of lag time, or people trying to talk over each other. I hoped this one would be more organized.

"Gentleman, I have everyone connected now. I have informed Jerome, Casey, and Draven of the circumstances. We have come up with a tentative plan that I will outline, and the others will interject anything I may have forgotten. Then we will open things to questions from you guys." Leo's voice swirled around us from the surround sound speakers.

"Sounds good to me. How about you, boss?" Wyatt looked toward me.

"Yup."

"Good. Casey has agreed to redirect Rook and Jasmine to your location as they are the closest from her pride. If we need further back-up, she will be on call with Jonah and his team. Draven has alerted the local nest and will be arriving late tonight. He's currently in the air on his way. The local Master has not responded to him, so he will be handling the vampires on his own. He has informed us he is coming in, assuming they are hostile until he determines otherwise. Jerome is sending Jax and a couple of others to help with any medical needs that may come of releasing the pack from this curse. He also sent Talia with them to help determine the black magic used, and to work with the local coven to help break it. This won't be the easy mission I had envisioned. We still have The Resistance to contend with as well. You guys are on the ground there, is there anything else we need to know before we continue?" Leo left no room for anyone else to speak as he related all this to us.

"Mack and I will arrive after things have been secured, to help relocate any shifters that choose to," Casey added.

"That won't be necessary, I appreciate the offer," Leo replied, a bit of a growl in his voice.

"That wasn't an offer, just a statement, Leo. My family is helping you, Mack's pack is putting themselves out there for you, I WILL be there as well," Casey huffed

"Leo, man, I would give up if I were you. She'll show up no matter if you approve or not." We heard Mack in the background.

"What about the cubs?" Jerome asked

"We were going to drop them with you and Mom if that is okay. I had meant to call you one on one after this," Mack addressed Jerome.

"Of course, son." You could hear the smile in his voice.

"Gentlemen, and lady, I can tell my assistance is no longer needed on this particular call, and as I need to rest the next few hours to be fully prepared when we land I will say farewell. Wyatt, I would appreciate it if you or one of your men could meet me. I do not trust anyone in that area at the moment, least of all the nest that currently resides in my child's home." With a click Draven had released his end of the line without getting the assurance that Wyatt would be there.

"Rook should be arriving at the same time, and we have an SUV waiting for them, Draven can ride with them," Mack said. It was obvious he had joined Casey closer to their speakerphone.

"No, honey, that's not a good idea. He'll have Jazz with him, and I don't think she's ready to deal with the father of all vampires that close up. She's been doing well with her therapy, I don't want to set her back," Casey replied.

"No worries, guys, I'd be happy to go pick him up. No one will miss me from the club tonight," Wyatt chimed in.

"Great, is there anything else we need to know before this evening?" Leo took control of the call again.

To the surprise of everyone in the room Steven spoke up. "Yes, there is one more thing." His voice wavered with the effort it took to participate in a call with so many Alphas.

We all waited, Jerome gently encouraging him. "It's ok, Steven, I sent you for a reason, you see and feel things the others don't take into consideration. What do we need to know before we decide on a plan of attack?"

Steven took a deep breath and blurted out. "Sterling found his mate, and she works at the club."

Jerome, Mack, Leo, and Casey all spoke at once, and I chose that moment to leave the room and grab a shower. I was in no mood to discuss my potential mate with anyone. I closed the door to my bedroom and ignored the voices, all except one, and that one was mentally knocking on the pack bond.

"Yes."

"I didn't mean to upset you or anger you, but they needed to know she was important," Steven replied.

I knew Steven did what he thought was needed, and if I stopped and looked at the situation from a logical standpoint I would have done the same. But my emotions were a wreck, and I wasn't ready to let anyone know she might be my mate, fox said it was so, but I still couldn't believe fate would provide another after I lost my first mate so many years ago.

"I'm not angry, you did what you thought was best. I just wasn't ready to make the decision on whether she is my mate or not, she hasn't even accepted me. It's all confusing and now everyone knows. It's fine, I'll deal with it. Don't worry yourself." For the first time ever I closed the door on the bond, to Steven and everyone else in the pack. I needed to be completely away to think. Deciding against a shower I grabbed my leather jacket and yearned to take a good long ride on my bike, but she was back in pack territory. A walk would have to do. I shrugged into my jacket, grabbed my cell phone, and slid it into my back pocket. I left without saying a word to anyone, they were still on the call and didn't notice that I left.

My phone dinged with an incoming text.

Keys to the Ducati are in the bowl on your way out. Just don't scratch it or I will own you—L

I smiled and glanced in the bowl by the elevator doors, sure enough there they were. I grabbed it and headed to the garage. The security guard greeted me when I exited.

"The Ducati is in the corner, enjoy your ride."

"Damn, Leo's fast," I mumbled to myself, but followed his hand indicating which corner and found it. Sleek, black on black. No chrome for Leo, he doesn't like to stand out, and his vehicles wouldn't either. I inserted the key and cranked her over expecting the rumble I usually get with my bike. Instead of that deep Harley growl, she purred like a well satisfied lioness. I shook my head and leaned forward releasing the kickstand and slowly maneuvering out of the garage. It honestly didn't matter if people three miles away heard me coming, right now I just needed the open road, wind in my face, and connection with two wheels. This girl was going to give me that and more by the end of my ride I could tell.

I took off in no particular direction, just to get away. I turned down streets littered with trash, and the occasional homeless person huddled on a stoop. The windows of the buildings were covered with rusted bars in an attempt at security. I slowed taking in the scents around me, the stench of urine burning my nose. I found myself navigating to the block that Reana lived on noticing that her building and one other were the only clean ones around. I stopped outside her building and gazed up trying to find the window to her apartment, but no lights were on in any of them. The guards outside followed my movements with their gaze, but didn't engage in any conversation with me. Satisfied that she was well guarded if she was inside I gunned the engine and continued on. The only other vehicles on her street were the semis entering and exiting a factory a block away.

There was a dilapidated gas station on the corner that looked like they catered to the diesel big rigs than regular gas automobiles. The next block a market shared space with what used to be a barber shop and some type of clothing store. The naked mannequins still in the windows. I turned at the next stop and weaved my way out of the slums I had been in and headed downtown. Exploring the city that we were attempting to protect from the evil trying to invade. The closer I got to the epicenter the more people were out milling about clueless to the filth located only a few streets from them. Neon signs advertised the newest rage in coffee shops, bars, and eateries. Traffic picked up, and I followed it out of downtown to the interstate that skirted the city.

My inner struggle took over, and driving went on autopilot as I followed the flow. I hadn't expected to find my mate when I took on this mission, and now I had to focus on the task at hand instead of her. My animal instincts fought the human inside me. Fox and I debated how we were going to handle things from here. Back-up was on its way, and I told him we could keep her safe until this was over, but we couldn't pursue her. We had to watch and protect from afar. My heart sped up with the knowledge I would have to keep her at a distance. I couldn't touch her or taste her until she was completely safe.

The mating urge was strong, but I needed to bottle that up and lock it away. I didn't have time to be distracted. Distraction is when mistakes occurred, mistakes led to death, and I couldn't handle the death of another mate in my lifetime. The fates had gifted me this chance and I would not take it lightly. The sun began to fade, and I exited the interstate turning back onto the ramp heading toward the city again feeling refreshed, and with a renewed sense of duty.

I had ridden all day, weaving in and out of streets, getting lost a couple of times, but ending up back at the club at dinner time. I parked across the street and watched as another SUV, exactly like the one that that we had borrowed from Ricky, pulled up to the door to deliver an employee. Fox perked up as soon as the back door opened. This particular vehicle held Reana within, I could tell her scent from a distance already. I paid attention to the way she exited, and how she interacted with her driver. She didn't have any indications of distress, so I sat back, knowing she would be safe inside. Fox on the other hand wanted to grab her, throw her on the back of the bike, and take off. I smiled, a great dream as it was, and the man in me knew it would jeopardize her job and the mission we were on.

My phone vibrated in my back pocket, and I answered without looking at the screen. "Yeah, Sterling here."

"You need to watch your mate carefully at the club tonight if you wish for her to survive. His witch has figured out who you are, and plans to destroy the club, and the pack within it."

"Who is this? Talia, is that you?'

"Yes, but you don't have much time, warn Reana, don't alarm anyone else. We are going to try and stop Ricky's witch, but I don't want to put your mate's blood on my hands if we don't succeed. I can't tell you any more than that."

"Who is she, who is this witch?"

"It's Tomas's head witch, she didn't perish in the fight as we thought. She escaped and sunk her evil claws into Ricky. She took her time and chose him for a reason. That reason I don't know, but now that she knows why you guys are here she won't hesitate to wipe the slate clean to start again somewhere else. I'm with the local coven, and we have convened some of the most powerful witches with us. I need to go prepare. Sterling, keep her safe if you want a chance to win her heart." Talia hung up on me.

I didn't hesitate. I strode over and threw the back door open, surprising the guards on each side. *No one would threaten my mate. Ever.*

The smell of food hit me as I walked down the stairs, the sounds of people followed. I descended the stairs and found a room set up as a makeshift cafeteria down the hall to the left of the club entrance. I knew Reana was in there, her scent of vanilla and something smokier wrapped around and led me to the doorway. I leaned against the doorjamb and watched her. Fox was bothered because she wasn't eating, just pushing her food around and taking small bites every once in a while. I knew the moment she sensed me, her back stiffened and she slowly looked over her shoulder. When our eyes met the rest of the room fell away. I saw nothing but her golden eyes, shining in the light, and framed by a cascade of hair she had yet to pin up. It felt like we had stared at each other for hours in those few moments, and I felt a slight shift in my heart, a piece falling back into place that had been missing for years. She broke eye contact first and rose taking her plate to the cart of discarded dishes.

She gathered her belongings and walked my way stopping in the doorway to gaze up at me. "What are you doing here?" she whispered.

"Just waiting for you." I smiled, lost in her gaze. I longed to brush her hair behind her ear and run my fingers along her neck to see if she felt as soft as she looked. Her scent became stronger and tinged with sexual arousal. She couldn't deny the attraction between us, deep down she felt it as strongly as I did.

"Are you going to follow me all night?" She quirked an eyebrow.

"As much as I would love to, no, I won't. I have other things I must attend to, but if you will allow me I would like to walk to into work." I shifted to allow her to walk through the doorway.

I thought I saw a hint of disappointment in her eyes before she looked away and strode through the door. I placed my hand on the small of her back as we walked, enjoying the fact she allowed that small contact. Her skin heated, and I could feel it through her blouse. Tonight she had on a white silky top that was thinner than the cotton blouse she wore last night. Fox preened at the thought she wore it just for us, allowing us to feel her skin even with that small barrier between us. I imagined the feel of it against my chest, heightening the anticipation of revealing what lay beneath it.

Our mating wouldn't be quick, I would savor every moment, every touch, and every taste with her. Just the thought had me adjust my jeans as my body reacted. I leaned down to her ear, my hot breath fanning her hair. "If you need me tonight all you have to do is say my name, I'll hear you, no matter where I am."

She stopped and looked up at me. "How will you hear one small word over the chaos that will be happening?"

"Because your voice will always be louder than anything else. I will hear you, trust me." I dropped my hand as my phone vibrated again. I pulled it out of my pocket and glanced at the screen. "I need to take this, remember, just say my name." I turned and walked into the hallway again to answer the call.

"Sterling?"

"Yeah, what's up?"

"The packages are secure and we are on our way," Wyatt informed me.

"Great. I'm at the club, I'll meet you outside."

"We just have to deliver one and then we'll be there," Wyatt replied, and the call went silent.

I ascended the stairs to await them. I decided it was in my best interest to move Leo's bike closer to the club. It wouldn't do to find Reana, only to lose my life because Leo's precious Ducati got damaged, or worse yet, stolen. I parked the bike against the building and informed one of the guards to keep an eye on it. He laughed until I told him who it belonged to. I didn't expect Leo's name to have that much weight here, but the look on the vamp's face told me different.

"Interesting," Fox commented.

I leaned against the building and waited.

CHAPTER 12

REANA

WHAT THE HELL *was he doing here?* That was my first thought when I saw Sterling standing in the doorway. Then his eyes caught mine and I couldn't look away. My inner fox jumped for joy, but I had no time for him or anyone she thought was our mate. Though she had never said that word to me before. His scent carried over everything else in the room. He smelled like how I imagined the forest smelled deep in its heart. Earthy and fresh at the core, and musky on the edges. I could taste it the longer I gazed at him. My appetite for food was completely gone, and I knew I couldn't put off the inevitable interaction, so I deposited my plate full of uneaten food and prepared to face him.

My mouth salivated the closer I got to him. My sex throbbed for his touch as I looked into his eyes again. We exchanged words but they didn't register in my mind, fox screamed for me to reach out and touch him. See if he felt as tough as he looked, or if he was softer than his demeanor. I held back. He stepped aside and allowed me through placing his hand on my lower back as we walked down the hall. I could focus on nothing else. The musk in his scent deepened, and I took that to mean he was as aroused as I was. My breasts began to ache, and I knew if I didn't get away from his touch I would be cleaning my thighs before shift, my panties were already damp.

I didn't have time for this hiccup in my life. Mates were like signing my own death certificate. I learned that even though Ricky says he wants the best for us and our pack, he doesn't want his "girls" to be anything but that. Single sells more beer, single sells more private shows, and single brings in the money. The moment you find your mate you may as well lie down in your own grave. I watched it happen firsthand, and I still miss Tammy desperately. I was going to learn from her mistake. No mates for me. A fling every now and then to ease the sexual need was fine, but mates were not. I took a few deep breaths as I pulled away from him, trying to clear my sinuses, but that only pulled his scent deeper into me.

We exchanged words again and again, I didn't really hear what each of us said until his last statement.

"Because your voice will always be louder than anything else. I will hear you, trust me." He dropped his hand as I heard the vibration of his phone. He pulled it out of his back pocket and glanced at the screen. "I need to take this, remember, just say my name."

I admired the way his pants hugged his ass as he walked through the door. I released the breath I had been holding in a whoosh of air. Damn that man was sexy as hell, and my hormones couldn't take much more. I had to stay away from him. I reminded my fox what happened to Tammy again, and she finally cowered down in a corner of my mind. The fight was strong in us, strong enough to fight a mating need that would soon be discovered.

Shaking off my emotions as much as possible, I put on my game face and began prep work for another long night in the club. Tonight was ladies night, which meant we would be twice as packed as normal. This night is when all the adventurous human women would gravitate to this side of town. Some excited, and others being drug by the one fun and oblivious female in the group. Free cover charge and drinks always brought them out in droves which lured the men to follow and made us one of the most popular clubs on a Tuesday night.

My coworkers slowly made their way in and we settled into our routine. We had done this for so long we worked together like a well-oiled machine—no talking or direction needed—we all had our duties and stations. The club was ready a good half hour before opening, and Suzy and I were prepping serving trays with shooters, napkins, tip jars, and anything else we might need to navigate the throng of people. I thought back to Sterling's comment that all I had to do was say his name if I needed him. My lips quirked in a smile as I realized that was meant to comfort me, but actually sounded more like a challenge. I decided I was going to prove him wrong—even without heightened senses, the noise of tonight's crowd would drown out anything I might try to say. *Challenge accepted, dear Sterling, I'll say your name tonight and prove that you won't hear me, no matter what you think.*

"Everyone ready?" Sam yelled. I turned with Suzy toward the door, tray in hand, heels high, and smile plastered on my face as he opened the doors and the crowd flooded in. They were lined all the way up the stairs, and I knew the line would extend outside and around the block, and would for the rest of the night. The rundown neighborhood wouldn't put anyone off tonight, we would be hopping till the last patron had to be escorted out.

In moments the room's temperature skyrocketed, and sweat began to bead and run down my back. It was that moment I regretted not bringing my extra cotton blouse. I didn't know why I had overlooked my normal routine but I had. Now I would be stuck with this one clinging to my skin all night encouraging the patrons to look and attempt to touch. The crowd ebbed and flowed around us like the waves in an ocean and Suzy and I stuck together so we didn't get caught in the current. I brushed up against way too much exposed skin, but again, that all came with the job. On nights like this fox holed up in a corner of my mind and hugged her tail around herself. Neither one of us liked being in big crowds. When you add in the drunks and supernatural wannabes, nights like tonight were rough.

I had learned over the past year how to handle it, barely, and I was good at my job. Tonight though, Sterling's voice became a distraction. I thought I heard him everywhere, a constant hum in my ear. The low tenor of his voice vibrated over my skin. I tried to locate him every chance I got, but it wasn't until my first break that I was able to really search. I found him on the second level standing with another shifter I hadn't met. He was talking, but his eyes were focused on me. His friend followed his gaze, slapped him on the back, and moved on. Sterling never let his gaze leave mine. He leaned both muscular arms on the railing. *"I told you I would be here if you needed. Everything ok?"* I saw his mouth move, and heard his words as if he were right beside me, but my mind couldn't wrap around that. The noise in here should have prevented that. Even without the crowd the distance between us would have been too far to have heard him. If I could hear him, then that meant he could hear me, right? So I gave it a try.

"Yes, everything's fine. I don't understand how I can hear you though. You sound like you are right beside me."

"I wish I were. I can be if you need." His eyes lit up. Yes I could see that, too. The club surrounding us faded into the background as I continued to focus on just him. *"From what I know, this is part of what confirms that we are mates. It is hard to explain, and I don't really want to in this crowd. But if you have time after your shift I would like to talk."*

"OK," I answered. *"But just talk."*

"Rea, break's over!" Sam yelled from the

other end of the bar. I looked at the bottle of water, still unopened in my hand, and realized my fifteen minutes had been spent staring at the one man I needed to stay away from. I twisted the cap off and quickly guzzled the cool refreshing liquid. Grabbing my refilled tray I joined Suzy back in the fray of customers. We still had six hours to go before we could start pushing people out the door. Six hours for me to figure out how to get out of talking with Sterling. Six hours until I knew I would fail at that.

My heels slipped on some type of wetness on the floor, but I righted myself before I lost my tray, and my ass. The first time in my two years of working here that I had lost my footing. I blamed Sterling for distracting me to the point I was unable to focus on where I walked.

"You ok, Rea?" Suzy asked with concern.

"Yeah, I slipped. Must be time to re-sole these heels. The tread is wearing off, and on a night like tonight I need all the traction I can get." I laughed her off and continued on. My tray emptied quickly, and as I turned to go load it up again Ricky stepped into my path.

"Reana, you have been requested for a private room on the second floor. Please go freshen up and join the club members in room six." He stared at me with his black beady eyes.

"Oh, hey, Ricky. Umm, I don't do the private rooms, remember. It's specifically in my contract." I looked at the floor and tried to go around him to fill my tray. He grabbed my arm and stopped me, and the stench of his breath made me want to gag. I knew better though, and swallowed it down.

"You will do as I tell you. I have some high rollers upstairs and they specifically asked for you. I don't know why, but they did. I tried to suggest some of the more endowed and loose waitresses, but they were adamant about it being you. Now go take off that nasty sweat-soaked top, put on a fresh one from the closet, and get your ass upstairs, or you're fired." He squeezed my arm hard and let go with a slight push toward the bar.

Sterling materialized as I took a deep breath, holding back the tears that threatened to fall. "I'll kill him," he growled.

I smiled. "You can't, not yet." I took another settling breath. "I'm fine, Sterling, go back to where you were." I didn't look at him as I made my way to the locker room. Sam quirked an eyebrow as I set my tray down and kept on walking. I shook my head side to side telling him not to worry. In the women's locker room was a closet that held extra pants, skirts, and blouses in a variety of sizes. I grabbed a plain white dress shirt in cotton this time and changed. The size was a little small, but it was the largest available. Ricky did that on purpose, keeping things at least one size too small, to entice the patrons, he rationalized. Personally I think he is a sleaze and just enjoys looking at our boobs and ass, the more he can see the better. A shiver ran down my back at my last thought.

I squared my shoulders, held my head high, and walked out and up the stairs to the second floor. I would not let this be the reason I lost this job, and I would not let any man or woman put their hands on me uninvited. I could serve this private room with dignity and respect, and keep my clothes on while I did it. Max greeted me from behind the bar as Sterling fell into step beside me.

"Hey Reana, room six requested you. I'm sorry." He dipped his head sheepishly. Max was a nice guy, and knew how I felt about doing the private rooms. "I tried to talk them into having Candie join them, but the girls wouldn't hear me."

That stopped me. "The girls?" I tilted my head.

"Yeah, it's a group of seven or eight guys and two girls. They seem ok. None of them have

ordered any drinks yet and they seem respectful."
He shrugged his shoulders.

"Ok, thanks, Max." I walked down the hall,
confused as to why girls would demand me. I put
that thought out of my head and opened the door
to room six with an air of confidence I didn't feel.
The stage with its pole stood vacant in the corner
and I prayed that I wouldn't be asked to dance for
them. The bar in the opposite corner sat empty of
a bartender, which was unusual. Most parties had
a dancer, a bartender, and at least two servers.
I glanced around and found that I was the only
server in the room. My eyes landed on the man in
the corner, and recognition hit me. He smiled and
walked toward me.

"Welcome, Reana. We hope we didn't scare
you too much by insisting you be our server, but
we wanted to talk to you." He nodded to the rest
of the people in the room. "These are my friends
and mean you no harm. Sterling, she's safe with
us, will you sit and join us?" Miguel, the one who
had chatted with me last night and had been part
of the four who gave me a ride home, a friend of
Sterling's, indicated a plush chair for me to sit in.

"Yes, please join us. Relax and rest your
feet if nothing else," one of the females added. She

was sitting on the lap of a muscular shifter, scruff covering half his face, his arms lovingly wrapped around her, giving comfort and protection at the same time. His eyes radiated love as he stared at her as she spoke. His gaze turned to me and his smile was welcoming.

"Please sit. We are here at Sterling and Wyatt's request and hope you can give us a little bit of insight to the pack. My name is Rook, and the lovely lady sitting with me is Jasmine." He squeezed her and she giggled. "You already met Miguel, and over there on that chair is our Alpha, Casey, and her mate Mack." I looked toward the other couple entwined together and both nodded their heads in hello.

I sat on the edge of my chair waiting. There were still two men standing at the back of the room that hadn't moved yet. Rook cleared his throat to get my attention again.

"Behind me on my left, your right, is Jerome. He is Alpha of the Black Mountain Pack, Sterling's Alpha. And next to him is a very dear close friend to both pack and pride, Leo." Jerome gave me a smile, but Leo's expression never changed, and he seemed to fade into the shadow even more. "Leo is one of the few shifters who still hides his nature around humans. Please keep the knowledge of what he is here in this room." Rook gazed at me, his eyes intense.

"Of course," I stammered.

"Great, the rest of our group will join us shortly. Wyatt and Steven are taking turns being seen in the crowd so that Sterling can be with us, and Talia, our witch friend, will be here as soon as she can, but she instructed us to start without her. Would you like something to drink while we wait on the rest?'

"No thank you," I squeaked out. Still trying to wrap my head around the group of shifters in front of me. Instinct told me I could trust them, well most of them. I wasn't sure about the one introduced as Leo. My fox hid in fear from him urging me to stay still and not bring attention to ourselves. I could feel he was a predator, and a large one at that. His eyes spoke volumes. Years of knowledge hid behind them and he commanded a room even leaning against a wall as he was. The three piece suit added to his air of authority. Blonde hair cropped short to his head, golden eyes, tan skin, and a stance of arms crossed, wide legged readiness rounded out Leo.

I moved on from him to check out Jerome.

He had a more approachable fatherly look. Brown hair silvering at his temples and warm brown eyes. I would guess him to be six foot tall, with what Tammy would have called a "dad bod," not super ripped, but still defined with a bit of cushion. Someone you could curl up next to and feel safe. His jaw was freshly shaven, and he wore comfortable jeans and a crisp polo. He held himself as I imagined a true Alpha would, his power radiated off him. You could tell he had been around for a while, and expected those he met to acknowledge his position.

I examined Rook and his mate, envying the closeness they shared, though they weren't as touchy feely as Mack and Casey. I noticed Rook kept his arms around Jasmine's waist, one hand holding hers and caressing her fingers. Her back was straight as she tried to lean into him, but the motion looked awkward and forced. They had a story, and I could tell she had a damaged past. I hoped they could work through it, because strong mated couples were needed in the shifter world these days. Rook looked former military with his khaki shirt, camouflage pants, and black military issue boots. His overpowering look was finished with a knife strapped to one thigh and a gun at his hip. Even with all that his eyes were kind when they met mine, and full of love as he gazed upon his mate. Jasmine was dressed for comfort, leggings and tank top covered with a short leather jacket. No jewelry adorned her, and her hair was cut in a short bob, the color what I would call platinum, almost white. When she turned toward me, here yes were a deep amber color, and held an echo of pain behind them.

Mack and Casey had eyes for no one but each other. This couple was different, as she was the Alpha of her own pride and he stood beside her. I had never met a male who would step aside and let a female rule, especially when his own father was Alpha of the biggest pack in America. She radiated compassion, yet she held an underlying thread of power that I imagined she could pull on when needed. She was on the thin side, but not weak, her arms were corded with muscle beneath her short sleeves, and her skinny jeans flowed like butter over her legs. Sensible tennis shoes adorned her feet. She had long curly hair held back with a clip, and a face that was a bit rounded. Her eyes grabbed mine and smiled, her animal shone through for a minute, but I didn't fear her, instead I felt safe and protected. She smiled fully, and I found myself relaxing and smiling back.

Mack constantly had a hand touching her somewhere, rubbing her hand, tracing patterns on her arm or thigh, keeping a constant thread between them. He had dark hair, a bit shaggy, tanned skin, and was dressed similar to Rook down to the gun and knife.

I cleared my throat. "How did you guys get weapons past the guards? This is supposed to be a weapon-free environment." If the guards were this lax, who knew what could be floating among the crowd downstairs?

"A simple cloaking spell got them past your guards. They are on us just in case. We have no plans on leaving this room until closing so you have no need to fear. Your Alpha is aware, he isn't happy about it, but knows better than to start a war with two of the biggest Alphas on this side of the continent," Jerome answered, his voice deeper than I expected, with a warm undertone that felt like a blanket wrapping around me as he winked at Casey.

"I appreciate the compliment, Jerome, but I have a lot to learn before I can deem myself one of the strongest." Her love for the older Alpha flowed through her words. This was a close knit group, and that was evident in how they spoke to each other and their body language toward one another.

Another person joined us through the back door of the room. The door usually used by staff. He kept his eyes on the floor as he addressed the room. "Talia has messaged saying she and her friends are ready. I recognized him from the group with Sterling, Steven I think was his name.

Jerome confirmed my assumption when he responded. "Thank you, Steven. Would you like to join us?" He indicated the sofa and chairs. Steven kept his eyes on the floor as he made his way toward us. He stopped next to my chair.

"May I sit beside you?" he whispered. Knowing that with all the heightened senses everyone in the room heard his question.

I didn't want to offend either Alpha in the room so I nodded. "Of course, you may sit anywhere you like. Can I get you a drink?" I felt awkward sitting and not doing my job. I went to stand, and he placed his hand on my wrist. His touch calmed me immediately. It's like his fingers sucked out all the nervousness that I had, and I looked at him, my eyes round with surprise.

"That's not necessary, Miss Reana, I'm fine." He smiled.

Jerome came forward, his comforting aura

wrapping around me. "Reana, Steven is a very special beta in my pack. Not many know of his special talents he just shared with you. Steven can bring calm and equilibrium to any member of the pack. He can take away pain, reduce nervousness, and even dull the mating urge with a simple touch. This is not a talent we want to make public." He placed his finger under my chin raising my eyes to him. "Do you understand?"

I hadn't realized he had gotten so close, I was just happy that for the first time I could remember I was completely at ease. "Of course. I would never betray your confidence." Jerome released my chin and I looked at Steven. "Thank you, your secret is safe with me, I promise."

He blushed slightly. "I know, it's why I chose to help you. You have a good heart, and since you are Sterling's mate, I knew my secret was safe with you."

"That's her?"

"What! When did he find his mate?"

"That explains a lot."

Comments began flying around the room at Steven's declaration. I held my hands up. "Wait, just wait." No one seemed to even remember I was there. "HEY!" At the sound of my raised voice all eyes turned toward me. I shrank back a little rethinking my outburst, but stopped myself. I straightened my spine and put on my big girl face. I was no victim, and no meek little female. "I am no one's mate. Sterling's fox seems to think I am, but I've only known the man for a day, and I can promise you I will not be mated to anyone. Not now, not anytime in the near future." I crossed my legs and folded my hands in my lap.

The room erupted with conversation again, all discussing Sterling, and the fact that the fates had brought him another mate, a second chance. I rolled my eyes and sat back fully in the chair letting them debate amongst themselves. I knew the truth, and they would find it out in time. As I watched their animated faces the little hairs on the back of my neck stood at attention and his scent greeted my senses. Sterling had arrived.

"It's so good to find my pack mates in a heated discussion about my personal life." His velvety voice wrapped around me as he spoke. "Let me get the answers to your questions out of the way so that we can focus on the task at hand."

I felt his hand rest on my shoulder as he stood behind my chair. I controlled my urge to rub my cheek against it and sat as still as possible. That simple touch sent shocks of awareness through my body. My breasts became more sensitive to the material of the bra encasing them. My thighs quivered with want and wetness began to pool between them. I hoped he would speak quickly and move away. Instead he squeezed my shoulder slightly, in support or acknowledgement that he could sense my desires, I didn't know.

"Yes, fox has told me from the moment I set eyes on Reana that she is to be our mate. But we all know how fate likes to throw us curveballs. I have been mated once before, and lost her. I had accepted that I would be living the rest of my life alone. I want to take the time to get to know Reana and her fox, but right now is not the time. She is in a tenuous position within this pack, and my first priority is to keep her safe, and rid this pack of the evil winding through it. When that is accomplished, and only then will I ask her to look inside and follow her heart and her fox. What happens after that is unknown. So please, let's table this discussion for another time when danger isn't breathing down our necks."

Someone's phone rang and broke the moment. I allowed myself to finally look up at Sterling. He met my eyes with a soft smile on his lips. No words needed to be exchanged, I knew he would give me the space and time I needed. We all turned as Leo's voice rang out. "Yeah." Breaths were held waiting for his next words, the anticipation thick in the air.

"What are we all waiting for?" I whispered.

Sterling knelt down and leaned toward me. "To see what information Leo will share with us. He is a man of few words as you will find out." He nuzzled my hair a moment, and then went to stand with Jerome as they waited to hear what Leo had to share.

"You are certain?" Leo stepped away from the wall and started pacing. "Yes, she's here, I'll see what information she knows. What's your ETA?" Leo ended the call and turned to face me.

"That was Talia, the witch I brought with us from the coven that works closely with Jerome's pack. She says the magic this witch uses is getting into the pack members and vampires, either through a type of injection or ingestion. Do your pack members have regular inoculations that you have to take?"

"No, we have never had to go to any doctor regularly." I shook my head.

"How about a communal kitchen?' Leo

MIRANDA LYNN

continued.

"Well, yeah. There is a small cafeteria here that always has breakfast, lunch, and dinner for those that can't afford food, or just don't want to waste their money on it. I don't eat there, as I prefer to cook my own food."

"But I found you there today," Sterling corrected.

"Yes, but I only nibbled on some bread, and didn't really eat any of the food. I went because I had no food in my apartment. Most of the employees do eat there though."

Leo continued to pace. "That's how she's getting to them. She is spelling the food. But that still doesn't explain the vamps. They don't eat human food."

The others started debating how that would happen when it dawned on me. "The appetizers."

"What did you say?" Sterling asked as he walked back over to me.

"The appetizers we provide free to all patrons, they are cooked by the same chef in the same kitchen. The vamps drink from donors, right? Well, those donors have to eat to replenish their energy, and I am sure many of them eat the free food here."

STERLING

Sterling stared at me in awe. "You are amazing." He grabbed my face and kissed my forehead before jumping up and getting everyone's attention. "Reana has figured it out."

I found nine sets of eyes on me once again. Leo was the only one to speak up. "And what did she figure out?" Sterling shared my revelation, and I could see the pieces fall into place on each face. "That's actually a brilliant plan if she's right," Leo replied. "Talia will be able to tell us if the spell would transfer through blood." Leo strode over to me and knelt placing his face on the same level as mine. "Reana, you are proving to be an amazing asset, and if you deign to approve of Sterling as your mate, you would be a much welcome addition to the company and my small circle of friends."

My mouth dropped open in shock. This larger than life man, this shifter who commanded a room simply by being in it, had taken the time to acknowledge that my theory had merit. I know they hadn't introduced him as an Alpha because he still stayed hidden in the human world, but I felt at that moment he could take any pack or pride he chose if he wanted. "Thank you, Mr. Leo, your words mean more to me than you'll know. As for Sterling, we will just have to see where things go."

Leo laughed. "You can call me Leo, no Mr. needed." He patted my knee as he stood up. "You have your work cut out for you, my friend. Take care with how you treat her, no matter which road she chooses."

"Her care will always come before mine, and above any others in the pack," Sterling stated, gaining approving nods from each male in the room. Putting my head further into a spin I didn't know if I could pull myself out of. Each word he uttered touched me on a deeper level, and I only had a few more layers before this man would be speaking straight to my heart. The fact that he could do that with a few simple touches and heartfelt words made him even more dangerous than I thought.

Casey broke my train of thought when she asked the question, "When will Talia get here?"

Wyatt smiled as a knock sounded on the door that led back to the club. "That should be her now. Reana, would you let her in please?"

I stood, straightened my skirt, and went to open the door giving the appearance of doing the job Ricky sent me in here to do. I stepped back and let in a tall thin wisp of a woman fully cloaked in a green hooded overcoat. She turned to me as I closed the door behind her reaching her hand out to touch mine. "May I?"

"Yes."

She closed her eyes as her fingers lightly touched the back of my hand. She breathed deep three times and was done. Her eyes opened, pulling her hand back to untie the bow at her neck removing her cloak. "She's completely untouched by magic." Her eyes glowed a dark green as they met mine. "It's a pleasure to meet you, Reana, I am Talia, and it's time we rid your pack of the evil trying to take over. Are you willing to help?"

"Anything to get the scum that has leached in out." I covered my mouth. Those were the words in my head, but I had not intended to speak them aloud.

"Good." She turned and floated the rest of the way into the room. "What have you discovered, Jerome?" She looked back to see me still standing at the door. "Reana, would you be so kind as to go get us a kettle and teacups? This calls for my special brew."

I was relieved to be requested to do my actual job, and went behind the bar in the corner filling the plug-in kettle to boil and arranging the requested cups on a tray. I could still hear the discussion, but was happy to have something for my body to be doing besides sitting idle. The room went from bottled anticipation to war preparation as they put their heads together to devise a plan.

Back in waitress mode, I made sure their drinks were always full and hot. The witch, Talia, had decreed that they only drink bottled water, or the tea she brought with her.

CHAPTER 13

STERLING

As EVERYONE BEGAN discussing the problem and how to safely deal with it my attention was brought back to Reana time and again as she went about her job. Her relief at being productive was evident, and her confidence in her abilities gave her a sexy appeal I couldn't deny. Behind the bar or carrying a tray she was in her element, knew the ebb and flow of customers' needs intuitively it seemed. A thought hit me, and I asked Talia why we were to only drink water or her tea.

"I can't say for sure if the drinks here aren't contaminated with her spell, so our best option is sealed water or my tea," she explained.

"Well, Reana has worked here for a year and not been effected by their drinks," I countered

"Wait, I don't drink, not the alcohol here anyway. Bottled water is all I ever have. I don't trust some of the bartenders here not to drug me, or double pour the liquor to get me drunk. I need all my senses in this job so I stay sober," she replied, removing empty bottles and replacing them with new cold ones.

That made sense, and pride swelled inside at how smart my mate was. She may look the part of sexy yet not so smart waitress, but beneath that beautiful head of hair was a brain that didn't miss a thing. "Talia, can you tell if the liquor behind the bar is spelled? If you could tell that Rea was clean by a touch, isn't it the same thing?"

"Unfortunately no, the spell changes when it hits living tissue and bodies. What the other covens and I have deduced is it's dormant until consumed. We think it's cloaked in a way, so that any magic detection that may be used will pass right over it when in liquid or solid form, but that's still just a theory. We need to get a sample of the food, cloaking spells cast on food are harder to do. Plus, here, where they have control over the food and who eats it their concern for detection is less." Talia looked at Reana, and I could see the wheels turning in her head.

"No, whatever you are thinking, Talia, the answer is no. I won't have you endanger Reana in any way." Standing to emphasize my point.

"Who the hell do you think you are? I get to

STERLING

choose what is dangerous to me and what isn't. I get to decide if I want to help. I have been in this hell of a pack for two years, and I get to choose if I do whatever it is she is going to ask me." Reana's face reddened with anger as she spoke. The color only highlighted the curve of her neck, and the dimple that had been hidden in her left cheek. I longed to caress both, my fingers clenching with restraint.

I ignored her, the need to protect my mate overpowering the sensible man who knew the next words out of my mouth would anger her even more. "Whatever you need, Talia, I'll get it. Reana needs to be kept as far away from suspicion as possible. If I could lock her in her apartment until this is done I would. The only reason I don't is the fact it would tip off Ricky, and ruin our chances of catching this evil bitch pulling his puppet strings." I avoided looking at Reana, not wanting to see the anger or even disappointment that may show on her face. She would understand in time fox assured me, I knew otherwise. That statement had erased any progress I had made with her. I would have to try and make her understand why I said it. If she let me, that is.

"Alright, asshole." She threw the bar towel she had been using to clean and strode toward

156

me. I didn't make eye contact until she stood toe to toe with me jabbing her finger in my chest." I don't know who the hell you think you are to come in here and decide what I can and can't do, or if I should be locked up like some weak pathetic excuse of a woman when you don't even know me. That shit stops now!" She whirled around her ponytail smacking my chest. "Talia, you tell me what you need and I'll get it. From now on, if you have thoughts of how I can help make sure you ask me, don't discuss it with Mr. Caveman behind me. I am not his mate, his property, or his to protect in anyway."

Her chest heaved with the breaths she was taking, her shoulders shook slightly with contained rage, and the flush of anger traveled down her arms. She was a spitfire, and at this moment I decided that fox was right, this little minx was meant for us and no one else. I gazed at the rest of those gathered as they watched her, admiration showing in their eyes, and grins of pride dotting their faces.

Talia sat up a bit. "Could you get us a sample of the food? Is it normal for the employees to take leftovers home?"

"Yeah, most of them do. It's easier than having to cook for themselves at home. I can do that," Rea confirmed.

"Great."

"But how do I get it to you? It would be suspicious if I took a detour to someplace I have never been on my way home."

I chimed in. "That's easy, I'll escort you home again, and you can leave it with me. I'll bring it back to the apartment where Talia can retrieve it."

"Like hell," Reana scoffed. "Who said you were taking me home?"

Leo added his thoughts. "That is exactly what needs to happen. Sterling has already made his interest known, so his continued pursuit of you will come as no surprise." He stood and stretched. "I would advise having a discussion with Ricky as a courtesy. Sterling needs to plant the seed that he wants more than a friendship, but don't go as far as to bring up the fact that you know she is your mate. If Ricky thinks that a woman has taken your eye, then he'll think you won't be watching him as much. It's a great cover for us as well. Reana being on the inside can help us acquire things we wouldn't normally be able to get." Moving toward Reana he addressed her. "As for you, watch yourself, and don't do anything that would put up red flags with any employee here. Continue as normal, accept the help we provide, and soon you'll be free of the evil here."

"I am confident you have things in hand. It's time for me to say my goodbye and end my visit so as not to bring any more suspicion to our group. Wrap things up here and disperse yourselves. The longer you are together the more suspicious it will seem. I will be returning to my office, but my resources are at your disposal." Leo left through the employee entrance at the back of the room.

"He really is a man of few words," Casey reiterated.

"Yes, but those few words have meaning, power, and purpose," Jerome added. "He has been there for me through times when I thought everything was falling apart and I couldn't make this pack last. His support and friendship has helped secure us as one of the most sought out packs to join. He believed in my dream, and believes in equality for all shifters. It doesn't surprise me he's willing to risk discovery to bring justice to those destroying this one."

Rook stood and stretched as well. "I think we need to table our planning until Talia can give us a report on if the food is where the magic is being introduced and re-established." He helped

Jasmine stand with him. "We need to leave the room at different times so as not to make it look like we were conspiring against Ricky. Jazz and I aren't up to the club scene tonight so we will take our exit out the back. The rest of you decide when to leave on your own. We will meet you back at the apartment Wyatt and the rest are staying at."

Steven stood and approached Jasmine. "May I escort you out?" An internal conversation flashed between their eyes and she accepted his offer. I noticed that he placed his hand on the back of her upper arm as Rook wrapped an arm around her waist to guide her out. Steven's shoulders slumped as Jasmine's rose. He was plying his magic touch once again. It worried me that he would give too much of himself soon, his need to take care of his pack overrode his self-preservation some days. I would have to make sure he took a good amount of time off after this mission to recharge and relax. I loved him for his devotion to the pack, but not when he jeopardized his own well-being.

Casey grabbed Mack's hand. "I want to dance, let's go check out the lower level."

Over the next hour everyone filtered out of the room till Reana and I were alone.

"You don't have to stick around, ya know. I

can clean up on my own." She huffed at me as she passed, loading her tray with the dirty teacups and half empty bottles of water.

"I know, maybe I want to stay because I enjoy your company." I crossed one leg over the other and reclined back in the leather club chair I occupied.

"Whatever. I can't finish my cleaning until you leave, and I still have a shift to finish downstairs." She rubbed at a perfectly clean spot on the bar for the third time since setting down her tray.

"No, you don't. We booked this room and your services as waitress for the full night. No shift to get back to for you." I smiled mischievously enjoying how she fidgeted. Her spunk had faded as each person had left, leaving only the nervous but still sassy woman before me.

"How am I supposed to get the leftover food you need if I don't finish out a shift downstairs? Those that work these rooms all night are expected to leave the back way, and pick their things up right before they head home. They don't stop in the club unless Ricky tells them to. Sam is the one who keeps the boxed leftovers in a fridge behind the bar. It would be extremely suspicious if I make a special trip to get them when I have never taken them home before." She kept her eyes averted as she spoke, focusing on cleaning all the table surfaces in the room. An obvious hint for me to leave.

"Then won't it be suspicious if you suddenly take leftovers, even after finishing your shift on the dance level?" I asked.

She stood, finally looking at me, and placed her hand on her hip. Exasperation radiating off her. "Sam always tries to push food on me, he thinks I don't eat enough, even though I always tell him I cook for myself. Since I came in early today and didn't really eat anything, when I accept this time he will see it as a final triumph. I'm Miss Follow the Rules most of the time, no reason to think I'm conspiring to take down the Alpha and his witch bitch." She waited for my response.

"Fine, I'll leave, but only because I do need to find Ricky and put my part of this plan into play. Remember, from here on out while I am here I will be taking you to and from work." I finally gave into the urge I had had all evening to run my fingers down the side of her face and neck, stopping at the opening of her blouse for just a moment, reveling in the feel of her silky smooth skin and the goose flesh my touch brought. The knowledge that a simple touch made her react so intensely stroked my ego. The self-satisfied smile I wore as I walked out the door spoke volumes to the guards and patrons that turned their attention my way. Ricky would hear about it before I ever tracked him down I know.

A small part of me, way back in my mind chastised myself for twisting perceptions that way. I ignored it, justifying my actions by reminding myself it was for her protection and nothing else. A lie if I ever knew one. This was the perfect opportunity to spend time with her and wear her walls down. She hasn't accepted me as her mate yet only because she isn't listening to her fox. She is denying her instincts, and I had a feeling it was because of something traumatic in her past. I wanted her to get to know me, the real me, not the one she sees now. The one focused on a mission, willing to do what is needed to eliminate a threat. I wanted her to get to know the man who owns a bar, cares about his employees, and enjoys the wind whipping around him as he rides his bike down the road. A man who has been longing for something more in his life for a while, and who has realized that something is her.

I leaned on the railing and looked down on the filled dance floor below picking out Mack and

Casey. I scanned the rest of the crowd, noticing that Mack wasn't the only on focused on his mate, about half the males, both shifter and vampire, were watching her with the same lust in their stances. Preparing to head downstairs in case they needed my assistance I saw Casey make a move that put everyone in their place without a word being uttered. She jumped toward Mack, who caught her immediately, wrapped her legs around him, and revealed her mark on his neck, licked it slowly, and looked up letting her panther shine through her eyes. I heard her growl ring above the chaos they called music. All eyes averted, and a few even bared their necks in submission. That wasn't a good sign, and I watched as Mack realized that. He began to carry her off the dance floor, a path opening to him as he headed toward the door. He looked up for a second and I inclined my head. The only acknowledgement between us.

Suzy, Reana's waitress friend, sashayed past me. "Suzy," I called out. She turned at the sound of her name. "Can you let Ricky know I need to speak with him?"

"I'm not sure where he is right now. You'll find him faster if you ask one of the guards." She waited for my response, licking her lips and giving me an appreciative once over.

"Thanks, I'll do that. Oh, and can you make sure Reana doesn't leave with her driver tonight? I plan to escort her home and don't want her sneaking away on me." I smiled and winked at her.

Her face fell but she agreed. "At least someone will get some action tonight," she murmured on her way down the stairs. I chuckled at her response and waved over one of the guards I recognized from last night and asked that he inform Ricky I would like to chat with him. I continued to observe from my vantage point knowing Ricky would find me in his own time. My body recognized Reana was amongst the crowd, a jolt ran along my skin, and my eyes followed her bouncing ponytail among the club goers.

She made a beeline for the bar, grabbing a tray and filling it with drinks, shots, and assorted items the patrons might need. How she maneuvered so well in those heels I didn't know, but she walked in them as if they were every day tennis shoes. She wove her way through the sea of people depositing drinks, smiling and discreetly pocketing tips as she went. Fox didn't like that she was near so many males. I didn't either, but I knew if I charged down there I would only push her farther away.

I had to trust that she could handle herself, and take comfort that I was able to watch over her if something turned sour.

The only time I got to see her fully was when she would hit the bar for refills. I relished those moments, seeing her pencil skirt skimming hips that moved like an ocean wave, her basic cotton button down blouse hugged breasts that were perky and full. This time when she went for refills she reached up and took her hair down. Last night it was in a bun, tonight I had noticed she only put it in a ponytail letting strands hang down to dust her shoulders. She shook her head and reached up massaging her scalp with her fingers for a moment before encasing those strands back in a bun at the nape of her neck.

Her neck, my fingers itched remembering how soft her skin was, and wanting to grace it again. I readjusted my stance to relieve the pressure the zipper in my pants was putting on the erection that was constantly at attention when I was around Reana.

"Sterling, so sorry for the wait, I had a small crisis to attend to." Ricky slapped my shoulder in greeting. "What can I do ya for?"

"Can we talk in private for a few minutes?"

I leaned down. "What I want to discuss is of a more delicate nature."

I knew my words had piqued his interest by the slight widening of his eyes. "Of course, room six is vacant now, we can use it." He and I both knew that was the same room I had just vacated. I followed him in and closed the door behind me. He made himself comfortable on the leather couch and looked up at me. "So, what's so delicate that we needed a closed door?" he asked, curiosity dripping from his words.

"It's about Reana, I wanted to officially notify you of my interest in her, and ask permission to actively pursue her." My words left a sour taste in my mouth. Speaking about her as if she were property was wrong in every manner. "I was told all relationships, whether for a night or longer, have to be approved by you. As you know, I don't plan on being around much longer, we have gathered enough information to report back to Leo. Wyatt simply needs a few more days to list the security measures he would recommend, and then we will be out of your hair. But until then it would be an added bonus to have a luscious female warm my bed for a few nights. My attraction drew me to Reana, so here I am, asking you, Alpha, for the go ahead." I continued to stand, since he hadn't invited me to sit, and I had to play the submissive in this encounter. Stroke his ego, take his suspicion off us and those that joined us tonight.

'Hmm, an interesting request, but Reana is a hard nut to crack. I'm not sure you could sweeten her to your bed in just a few days." Ricky got up. "I do have a few other girls I know would be most willing to accommodate you." He watched my face for any reaction.

I smiled in appreciation of his offer. "I have met a few of your girls, and Reana is the only one I have any attraction to. The challenge and the chase is sometimes more erotic than the actual act of bed play."

"Well, it will be a challenge, I assure you, but I think I'll enjoy watching this chase." He shook my hand and clapped my bicep. "Yes, you have my permission to try. I wish you luck, son, you'll need it." He laughed and left the room.

"Son, he dare call us son. Does he have any clue as to our age?"Fox growled at me. "Our age, that's what pissed you off about that whole exchange?" I shook my head as I exited the room. Some days I didn't understand his thought process, even after almost one hundred years he threw me for a loop with his crankiness.

CHAPTER 14

REANA

I FINISHED THE LITTLE cleaning needed in the private room calming myself as I did so. By the time I reached the bottom of the back staircase I was back in my normal kick ass waitress mode. I would not let that shifter get under my skin, no matter what he did. Focus, that's what I needed, to focus. On both my job tonight, and my job to help take down Ricky and his evil witch bitch. Fox giggled, she liked that nickname. The thump of the music reached me before I arrived at the door to the main floor. I pushed through and made a beeline straight for the bar to grab my tray and get back to work.

I felt the moment his gaze found me. The little hairs on the back of my neck stood at attention and the skin tingled as I remembered his touch there. Finishing my shift tonight was going to be harder than I anticipated if he chose to watch from above all night. Deciding to make him drool a little I added an extra flip of my hair as I turned and swayed my hips a tad more, which made the top button on my shirt stretch revealing the top curve of my cleavage. I knew he couldn't see it, but it gave me the extra confidence to flirt with the patrons while he watched. Another bonus to this was the tips that flowed into my hands the rest of the night.

Suzy caught up with me on a refill round. "Hey girl, how was the private party?"

"Fine, nothing special." Sam raised a bottle water to me and I nodded yes, grabbing it from him to quench my dry throat.

"Well I don't know what happened but the sassy girl that returned needs to stay. I've seen the tips flowing into your pocket. The patrons love it. This is how you make the money to get out of the dump you're in."

"You would be there with me if you weren't shacked up with one of the guards. At least you chose a shifter guard, but still, he is the only reason you aren't living in the dump apartments with me," I threw back at her.

"Ok, kitty, put away the claws. If I didn't already know your fox well I would guess you shifted to a cat of some sort." Suzy laughed at her own joke. "Anyway, thirsty drunks await, off to serve." She winked at me and disappeared into the crowd.

My wait was a bit longer as I actually had a couple specialty orders to wait on. I took my hair out of the ponytail I hastily put it in before shift. I normally wore it in a bun. The less you had that hands could grab the better. I ran my fingers through the length, making a mental note to go get a trim soon, and massaged the ache out of my scalp that always came with wearing it in a ponytail. I quickly twisted it into a bun at the nape of my neck and secured it with the ponytail holder I had. I preferred a flexi clip, but didn't have one in the apron I was wearing. Sam put the last order on my tray and I went back to work. A few steps away from the bar I realized the ever present feeling I had when Sterling was watching me was gone. I glanced up and he wasn't at the railing. A wave of sadness washed through me. *"Don't be sad, he'll return. Can't always watch us, our mate is important, and busy."* My fox tried to reassure me. I shook my head. I didn't have time to have a mental conversation with her right now. If she had her way we would have already hiked our ass up and offered it to him on a platter.

The rest of the night progressed without issue. I always knew when he was watching, but that's all he did. I should be happy that he left me to my job, but a tiny part wondered if his attraction was real, if his claim that we were his mate was true. I chided myself, I was getting what I wanted, to be left alone. My emotions just weren't on the same track. I missed the little flirtations, the feel of him close, and the small touches he had given me. I was concentrating on what I was missing that I didn't see the man step in my path. I couldn't stop in time and ran smack into him. It was near closing so thankfully my tray was empty, but by the glaze of his eyes he wasn't. He reached out as if to steady me, though he seemed to be the one who needed an extra hand. Swaying on his feet he grabbed my arm.

"Hey, sweetie, you need to watch where you are going," he slurred, the stench of his breath assaulting me.

"I'm so sorry, here, let me get you a drink on the house." I tried to remove my arm, thinking he really didn't need anymore drinks, but the idea of free usually worked to get me out of situations like this.

"Nah, honey, I'm done for the night, but you could make it up to me in other ways." He pushed closer to me, my tray pinned between us as his hand moved up my arm to my shoulder and his other found my hip in a bruising grip. "I have a private room paid for through closing time, and a little after if I need. Join me there and show me how sorry you are." He leered down at me, the stench of his stale sweat mingling with the death flowing out his mouth.

I breathed shallow but evenly, keeping my heartbeat calm. Any sign of fear set off men like this. The guards would see him soon and take care of it. I just had to keep him here, and keep him talking. "I appreciate the offer, but I need to finish up my shift. Would you like a coffee or water instead, and how about an order of wings, the kitchen hasn't closed yet." I smiled sweetly, gripping the edge of my tray.

"I'm not hungry for food, doll, and you know it. Now don't make this hard, I don't want your Alpha sticking his nose into my business. Turn around and walk slowly up those stairs, and everything will be fine. I'd hate to leave marks on your pretty skin." He trailed a finger down my throat to the opening of my shirt just above my cleavage. I couldn't help the shiver that ran down my spine at his touch.

"I need to put my tray up first and let my friend Sterling know I have to work late. If I don't he'll come looking for me." I went to move around him.

"No funny business, honey. Put the tray up, but no calling anyone." He let me pass, still keeping his grip on my hip and walking with me.

"If I don't, he will come looking for me. Sterling is the driver who takes me home at night, if he doesn't hear from me or my Alpha about a schedule change then his job is to find me." I was making things up as I went, and hoping what Sterling had told me earlier about hearing my voice above all others was true. I couldn't take this guy down by myself right now. If he were sober then yes, but drunk and already having a death grip on my hip it would prove harder. I placed my tray on the bar and smiled at Sam.

"Hey Rea, everything ok?" He came over, wiping the bar down as he stood there.

"Yeah Sam, can you let my driver Sterling know that I'll be a little late tonight and not to worry." I hoped Sam would get the hint without giving away anything. I should have never worried though, he went right along with it, but his eyes said 'I got you.'

"Sure thing, though Ricky may not be happy." He looked at the guy next to me. "You have gotten permission from our Alpha, correct? Nobody touches the girls without it."

Death Breath laughed and pulled me closer to his side. "Your so-called Alpha, Ricky, and I go way back, an unwritten agreement stands. I don't need permission from him for shit." He looked down at me, his eyes that of his animal. Wolf eyes. Not good. "Let's go, honey, I'm done waiting." The hairs on the back of my neck stood up, and a familiar scent broke through the smell of death this shifter radiated and I smiled.

We turned to find Sterling standing inches behind us. As much as I would have loved to kick this guy's ass, it would have jeopardized my job and position in the pack. I know, stupid right, but nothing in this pack was smart anymore. I chose to relax and watch him handle the scum next to me.

"Hello friend, I suggest you let go of Miss Reana. You've had a little too much to drink, and I am not comfortable with you taking any of our girls to your private room." Sterling stood, legs wide and arms loose at his sides radiating relaxation, but still prepared to fight.

"And who the hell do you think you are? You do know who you're talking to, right?" Death Breath puffed his chest, but his hold loosened just a bit on my hip. I could feel bruises beginning to form where his fingertips had been. I tried to move away from him slightly while his attention was focused elsewhere. I made it about two inches before his grip tightened again.

"I honestly don't care who you are, you are not allowed to touch any of the employees in that way. Please remove your hand from her before I remove it from your body." Sterling's nostrils flared with his declaration.

"Hey man, everything ok here?" Wyatt showed up just behind Death Breath, taking him by surprise.

"It will be when your goon here moves and lets me escort my girl here upstairs," Stinky replied. He thought Wyatt was there to help him out, how funny.

"Oh sorry, man, didn't mean to confuse you." Wyatt stepped closer and addressed Sterling. "We have a problem here? I've been itching for a bit of confrontation." He grabbed a hold of the wrist attached to the hand at my waist. I could feel heat through my shirt, and as I looked over my shoulder Wyatt's eyes were no longer his but that of his animal, and a small tendril of smoke escaped his nostril. He winked at me as his mouth widened into the grin of a predator. I looked back to Sterling who was now looking intently at me.

Wyatt's wink should have scared me, but all I felt was safety and comfort, the fingers at my hip began to release again, and in the next second I was in Sterling's comforting embrace, and Death Breath was on the floor, arm bent behind him, fingers almost touching his head and Wyatt's full weight kneeling on top of him. "You won't be escorting anyone tonight or anytime in the near future."

"Owww, get off me. That burns! You'll regret this, you have no idea who I aaaaa—" Wyatt cut off his tirade by pushing his face into the filthy floor. The smell of burnt flesh wafted to me.

"Wyatt, dial it back, Ricky is on his way down." His embrace loosened as he spoke to me. "Let me handle Ricky, you won't like what you hear, but please don't interrupt. Only answer questions directed at you, and I'll explain everything on the way to your place." His stance relaxed as he kept one arm draped over my shoulders and the thumb of his other hand hooked in a belt loop as he waited for Ricky to reach us.

"Do we have a problem here, gentlemen?" Ricky asked as he took in the scene in front of him.

"Actually we do, this asshole had his hands

on Reana without permission. We simply put him in his place, but I would appreciate it if you would also set him straight. I expect that during the duration of our agreement no other will touch Reana." Sterling's voice was laced with steel as he spoke.

Death Breath tried saying something, but it was muffled and only encouraged Wyatt to shove his face further into the floor, I'd be surprised if he didn't have a broken nose at this point. I didn't smell blood, but I couldn't smell much over the burnt flesh aroma. I tried to stay as relaxed as Sterling seemed, but listening to them discuss who could touch me and who couldn't rubbed me the wrong way. I was the only one who had a say in that—my body, my decision. I kept my mouth shut though, I wanted to see where this went.

"My apologies, I haven't had time to get the word out since our talk. I'm sure there was no harm meant. If you could release him we can clear up this misunderstanding." Ricky tried his best to be the voice of reason but his smile counteracted that. Wyatt let Death Breath up and stepped beside Sterling. He sprang up, tilting on his feet as he rubbed his nose with his good hand. The other arm hung limply at his side. "Jason, I've told you before you have to get approval through me to pursue any of my girls here."

"Bullshit, Ricky, you and I both know I've always had free reign, what's so fucking special about this one? And what are you going to do about that asshole? I think he broke my arm," DB whined.

Wyatt jumped in before Ricky could respond. "Nah, man, just dislocated your shoulder. I can pop it back in for ya if you want." He cracked the knuckles on each hand as if preparing.

"That won't be necessary, Wyatt." Ricky turned to DB. "You know the rules changed when I took over. I have overlooked your transgressions because the women you pursued were receptive to your offers. Reana wasn't, you should have stopped when she offered something besides herself, which I assume she did." Ricky looked at me for confirmation.

I gazed up at Sterling and he nodded for me to respond. "Yes sir. I offered free drinks and food as an apology for running into him."

"Just as I thought. Jason, if I know you as well as I think, you most likely put yourself in her path so she had no option but to bump into you," Ricky pushed.

Death Breath, I couldn't bring myself to

acknowledge he had a real name, avoided eye contact and muttered, "Whatever."

"That's what I thought. Well I am informing you here and now that Reana is off limits, and you are banned from the club for the next week. Go home, sleep it off, and think about how you want to handle the rules here. If you can't agree to the new terms keep yourself away permanently." Ricky waved for a couple of the bouncers to come forward. "Make sure Jason makes it home in one piece tonight, and put his name on the black list until I say otherwise." The guards stoically followed orders. When DB was out the door Ricky turned back to us. "I apologize, Sterling, I will make sure all are aware that Reana is off limits while you are here. Enjoy your pursuit, and I wish you the best of luck on conquering the ice queen here." He laughed and moved through the few people left in the club to the entrance to his private stairs.

I whipped around to face Sterling. "Permission to pursue…ice queen…conquest…" He placed his finger on my lips.

"Not here."

He was right, I knew that, but I was so pissed I didn't care. "Reana, I've got leftovers. You going to take any home this time?" Sam called out, and I knew that was my cue.

I turned on my heel and walked over. "You know what, Sam, I think I will."

"Really, I've never known you to take food home." He quirked an eyebrow.

"I know, but tonight I don't feel like cooking. I'm too pissed, I'd probably end up burning my apartment down. It's safer if I just heat something up."

"Our visitors got you flustered, foxy?" Sam laughed "I've never seen you so..." He leaned in and lowered his voice, "Be careful, if it's true feelings, you need to squash them. I don't want you ending up like Tammy."

I reached out taking the Tupperware container, and patted Sam's hand in the process. "Don't worry, I won't. These guys are only here for a short time, I can keep my distance until they leave. Remember, I'm the Ice Queen." Sam laughed as I turned to leave.

Suzy waved me over to the table she was wiping down. "Hey, boss says you can go home. You've had a hell of a shakeup. I got you covered, sweetie, go home and rest." She hugged me. "I'll see ya tomorrow."

I blew out a breath as I made my way back

to Sterling and Wyatt. Knowing that I was beat this round. "Hold this for me, will you? I need to go get my purse and coat from the locker room." I handed over the leftover container. They, of course, followed me like puppies. I stopped in the locker room doorway. "It's ok, I don't need your help in here. I know how to find my things on my own." Wyatt chuckled as the door closed. I grabbed what I needed, took a deep breath, and joined them once again noticing Wyatt was gone. Sterling placed his hand at the small of my back explaining before I could ask.

"He went to get the SUV for us. He should be waiting by the time we reach the outside door." His hand guided me up the stairs with just the slightest pressure, awareness of how near he was flushing through me. Reaching the exit he stopped me, took my coat, and handed the leftover container to the guard waiting to open the door for us. He held my coat offering his assistance to put it on. I turned and slipped one arm in at a time having to switch my purse from hand to hand as I did. He turned me around and slowly buttoned it for me. I never thought a coat could be used sensually, Sterling proved me wrong. He finished, took the container back from the guard, and held his arm out to me, elbow crooked for me to loop mine through. Acting the perfect gentleman. No smart remarks, no stolen touches, no heated gazes. I wasn't sure how to feel. Off balance obviously, happy that he was backing off, or disappointed that he wasn't trying harder.

Wyatt was outside by the SUV with the back door open. "Your carriage awaits, my lady," he bowed before me raising his head at the last minute and giving me one of his signature winks. All signs of his animal side gone.

I giggled. "Why thank you kind sir." I climbed in scooting over to give Sterling room to sit too. Wyatt closed the door and rounded the hood to reclaim the driver's seat. He had driven me home before so didn't have a need to ask directions this time. I buckled up and relaxed into the heated leather seat. Sterling placed the container of leftovers in the passenger seat beside Wyatt.

"I'll send those back with you. I'm sure Talia will want to get started on them as soon as possible," Sterling commented as he sat back.

"I assume you won't be returning to the apartment with me tonight?" Wyatt waggled his eyebrows.

"No, but not for the reasons you insinuate." Sterling reached for my hand and encased it in his warm one.

"Whatever you say, boss." Wyatt replied and turned on the radio. We rode the rest of the way to my apartment building without further conversation simply enjoying the music coming from the speakers. Wyatt turned the music down when we arrived. "Home safe and sound." He smiled at me in the rearview mirror. "You sure you don't need me to wait, boss?" He directed his question to Sterling.

"No, I'll be staying here tonight, we'll see you in the morning."

"Whoa wait just a minute there, bucko, who said you could stay?" There was no way in hell Sterling was staying the night.

"Your Alpha did." Sterling's eyes pleaded with me to be quiet. There was more to him wanting to stay than just getting into my bed. "It's for your protection," he added.

Okay, I'll admit the look he gave had me curious about his plans. I waved my hand shooing him out of the vehicle. I didn't say a word, just followed him out and waited while he closed the SUV door behind me. I smiled at the guards watching the building as Sterling guided me up the steps his hand once again gracing the small of my back. This man threw off the weirdest signals and I decided to pick my battles with him. I waited until we made it up the stairs and through my door before ripping into him.

"Now tell me what the hell is going on. I am not property that Ricky can just hand out willy nilly. I thought you were smarter than that, I thought you and your band of goons were here to help fix the shit hole that this pack has become, but now I'm not so sure." I paced behind the second hand couch that separated my kitchen and living room, my hands flittering about in agitation. "I am not some female to be given to the highest bidder or used as a reward for not messing with things." I continued to pace while Sterling leaned against the wall by my front door in a nonchalant manner. When he didn't respond I stopped and stared at him.

He pushed off and walked toward me until we were toe to toe and I had to look up to meet his eyes. "Are you done?"

"Hell no I'm not done," I huffed, but couldn't think of anything else scathing to say. Words flew right out of my head as his gaze intensified.

"I think you are." He smiled. "Now let me tell you the real reason I am here. It's exactly as I told Wyatt, it's for your protection, and I have your Alpha's permission to pursue you. If I simply dropped you off and left, that fact would get back to him and would raise suspicion. I made the fact that I wanted to get in your bed very clear when I spoke with him earlier. It was the only way I could think of at the time to keep you in the loop on what we discover and how we plan to move forward." He held his hand out to me, asking without words to trust him. I looked from his hand back to his eyes and saw he believed what he said. I placed my hand in his and let him lead me around the sofa to sit down. He let out a breath when we sat.

"Ok, now tell me how you being here with me all night helps with your group's plan."

"Wyatt will have given Talia the food you brought with you by now. She told us that it would take at least twenty four hours to determine whether it was spelled and another forty eight minimum to come up with a counter spell. Once she has that created we have to figure out how to get that either into the food or those affected without Ricky and his witch realizing it." He paused to see if I was following. I nodded for him to continue, I was holding off on an opinion until I knew the whole plan. "There is another who is joining us, and should already be at the apartment. You may not have heard of him but he's old friends with Jerome and I and he is the oldest vampire out there. Draven does not leave his home often, but when told of the situation here knew that his help would be critical to bringing down the evil that has taken hold and spread roots here. The Master Vampire in this area is one of his children so he has connections with all those working with Ricky and your pack. I don't know how they were spelled, but he will."

"I understand all that, but you still haven't told me how you being in my apartment with me figures into all this."

"If Ricky thinks I'm working on trying to get into your bed, then hopefully he'll think I won't have time to look any closer at what he's doing at the club, or elsewhere. He thinks I'm letting my lust for you drive my actions, and if he thinks I'm out of the way he won't work so hard at being the perfect Alpha, he'll make a mistake somewhere, and that's when we'll be able to catch him."

"And if you go home instead of stay here…" I prompted.

"One of his guards will report it before I get to the end of the block."

"But you're not actually going to sleep with me." I tilted my head, trying to decide if that thought bothered me or made me happy.

"Not if you don't want me to. I can sleep on the couch if you wish. I will ask that you leave your door open just in case my feelings about Ricky are wrong and he sees through my ruse. I have no doubt that he would eliminate you if he thought you were a threat."

Sterling was right that Ricky wouldn't hesitate to remove me if I became a problem. That's one reason I chose to keep my head down, do my job, and stay off his radar. It had been hard enough to get the "no private room assignments" added to my contract. That had put me on his radar for a good six months, kicking Sterling out of my apartment would bring me back to the top of his watch list. "Wait, you think I'd want you in my bed?" *Yup, that's what blurted out of my mouth.* I flushed with embarrassment and quickly rose moving to the kitchen going through the motions of making a cup of tea. Sterling didn't follow, but turned so he could see what I was doing.

"I'll be honest with you, Reana, because I think we both deserve it. Yes, I want to be in your bed, my fox wants to be in your bed, but neither one of us will go there without invitation. Yes, I hope you invite us, sooner rather than later, but we are willing and prepared to wait."

A comment that was said earlier came back to me. "Someone mentioned you had a mate before."

His face fell just a bit, his eyes took on a faraway look. "Yes, many many years ago."

"Then we can't be mates. You only have one true mate in your life, right?" That settled things, the feelings I had were simply attraction, and I could tamp those down easily enough.

"Fifty years ago I would have said yes, but I have seen things to prove otherwise. I never thought Fate would give me a second chance at having a mate and a happy ending. You are that happy ending, and I'm willing to wait for you as long as it takes."

Well hell, I didn't have anything to say to that statement, so I did the stupid thing and asked, "Will you tell me about her?" I mentally slapped myself as soon as the words left my mouth. Did I really want to hear about his amazing love, the mate he lost tragically? I didn't want to stir up those memories for more reasons than that. I realized that he would compare me to her, and I know I would be lacking in many aspects. At least this way he knew early on I was a waste of time. *"No, you are not. He can love us, and he does love us. He is mate.*

Just wait. His story is important, listen." I swear my fox chose the oddest moments to speak to me. We didn't have the greatest communication, and her English translations were rough, but she hadn't led me wrong yet.

"If you wish, yes, but you must join me on the sofa. Talking to you this way is putting a kink in my neck." He turned around, confident that I would join him, and he was right. My curiosity got the best of me. I filled two mugs with tea, put them on a tray with the sugar and milk, and joined him waiting for the story to start.

CHAPTER 15

STERLING

SHE WANTED TO know about my mate. She had died so long ago I felt that I had finally put that part of my life in the past. Reana had a right to know, being gifted a mate twice in a lifetime was rare and unheard of. If my mate wanted to know my story she was entitled to it. If I didn't tell her now she would eventually find out through the mating bond. When two mates complete the bonding process all memories are open to each other, there would never be secrets between us. She settled next to me with her mug of tea and patiently waited for me to begin my tale.

"Her name was Mia, and we met when we were both cubs. The pack elder knew we were destined to be mates before we did. We grew up together and formed a friendship that connected us deeply, we didn't realize that connection was the mate bond twining us together even before we matured enough to develop the sexual attraction as well. Our parents knew it, and made every effort to keep us together as much as possible." I took a breath, remembering all the things I had locked away after she died. "Our mating wasn't anything spectacular, it was just the next expected step for us. My father was the Alpha of our pack, though we called it a skulk since that was before the species mingled. Her father was his beta, so it just seemed natural that fate chose for us to be mates." I glanced over to gauge Reana's reaction so far. A happy smile graced her face and her posture had relaxed into the sofa cushions, but she didn't say a word, giving me the space to share at my own pace.

"Mia was kind, loving, and smart as a whip. But she was also submissive, and the most amazing mother I have ever known." I glanced out of the side of my eye to see Reana's eyes go round. "We had one kit, a little girl who looked just like her mom, and had the same open and loving heart. It took a long time for Mia to conceive, and due to complications of that delivery she was unable to bear anymore. Our daughter was seven when the shifters made the decision to reveal themselves to the human world. A few months after our village was raided by hunters. Only a few of us escaped through tunnels that had been built shortly after the coming out. Mia, our daughter, and myself made it to the end of those tunnels only to find more fighting and destruction. That's where I met Jerome, he tried to help us, but he and I watched our mates and family die right in front of us."

Reana gasped and reached a hand out, touching my arm in a gesture of comfort. I covered her hand with mine and looked into her eyes. Letting the pain I felt show. "It's ok, it's been a long time. The pain is still there, but I know they are in peace together."

"Sterling, I didn't know. You don't have to go on." She put her mug on the coffee table and scooted closer to me, moving my arm and draping it over her shoulders as she wrapped her arms around my waist hugging me. "I can't imagine having to go through that. I'm so sorry." She laid her head on my chest and squeezed. Her sweet scent wrapped around me in a warm hug, and I realized at that moment I never wanted to lose this feeling. With just a touch I felt loved in a way so very different than anything before. I kissed her hair and enjoyed the moment. She leaned back a bit and looked up at me. "Now this doesn't mean you get to sleep with me, but I want to thank you for telling me your story. She sounds like a wonderful mate, and I am so sorry that you lost her and your daughter." She pulled away and scooted back a bit, just out of reach of my arm. "I need to tell you something, too." She breathed in deep and looked away.

"I used to have a roommate. She was killed in a head on collision. Her mate was driving. Tammy was my best friend at the club which is why we chose to live together. She wasn't the brightest crayon in the box, but she made up for it with her love and loyalty." She looked at her hands, twining her fingers, a gesture I recognized as her way of keeping her nerves in check. "She came home right after Ricky had taken over, I didn't even realize he was Alpha yet. I was asleep when he defeated our previous Alpha, and the shift in the pack bond wasn't strong enough to wake me." A heavy sigh escaped her. "Ricky had been the manager of the club, and part of our contract with him is that we are to stay single, no mating, and no long term relationships. It's better for business. Anyway, Tammy came home all excited that Ricky had granted her request to complete the mating bond with her mate. They had found each other months before but had stayed away from each other as much as they could because of that contractual clause." She finally looked me in the eyes.

"I watched her and her mate die that night, and it wasn't an accident. I tried to warn her that Ricky was testing her, that she needed to really think about the way he worded his approval, but she wouldn't listen to me. They drove away and straight into the other lane in front of a semi-truck on the opposite side of the road." Her eyes glistened with unshed tears. "I saw someone in the road that night, cloaked in black, raising their hands as if controlling the vehicles, and I'm almost positive it's the witch bitch that Ricky is working with."

"That's why you don't want to admit that what we have between us is the true mating bond. You're afraid Ricky will find out, aren't you?" I scooted closer, fuck Ricky and his rules. My mate was sitting here in front of me, upset, and I'll be damned if I sit here and watch it. I pulled her into my lap, wrapped my arms around her and vowed, "No one will take you away from me, especially a jackass like Ricky. Alpha or not, he's only in that position because of the magic he's using. Give us a few more days to rectify that and then we'll take care of Ricky." I gently placed my finger under her chin raising her eyes to me. "Will you give us a chance if he's gone?"

She closed her eyes, "Yes."

It was whispered but I'd still take it. "Do you still want me to sleep out here on the couch?"

"I think it's best, everyone would be suspicious if all of a sudden I allowed you in my bed. I didn't get the title of Ice Queen for nothing." She giggled.

"Can I just sit and hold you for a while?" I didn't want to let her go, and fox was pissed that I even agreed to sleep on the couch. As far as he was concerned our mate let us in her home, which meant all access. I ignored him and just relished in the feel of her in my arms. The moment didn't last as long as I hoped as my phone rang in my back pocket. Rea went to move and I tightened my hold on her. "Whoever it is can wait."

"What if it's about the food or the vampires or something else?" She wiggled out of my grasp but not completely off my lap. "You need to check."

I knew she was right, but hated to burst the bubble we had created in that moment. I leaned to reach my pocket and pulled out my phone. One missed call from Wyatt. My finger hovered over the call button just as a text came in. I tapped the notification and opened it.

I hate to interrupt whatever you have going

on but Jerome wanted me to update you. Talia took the leftovers I brought to her connections and they have already discovered that yes indeed that's how the witch is spelling the members. They are diligently working on a counter spell and estimate having it ready within a day. Draven was unable to get his progeny on the phone and has gone to the local nest in person. Will update you when we know more. –Wyatt

I let Rea read with me and then sent a quick response letting him know we saw it and awaited further information. "I doubt we will hear much before morning." I knew that the intimacy we had shared only a moment before was gone. "You should probably get some sleep, if you have an extra pillow and blanket I'll bed down here." She stood brushing imaginary lint off her skirt.

"Of course, the bathroom is in the hall if you need." She took the tea items to the kitchen and disappeared into her bedroom. I heard her rummaging through things. I quickly washed up and relieved myself and was back on the couch by the time she returned with a pillow and blankets. "Here you go, I'm sorry the couch isn't more comfortable."

"It's fine, remember to leave your door open

just in case." I smiled taking the items she offered. "Sleep well."

"You, too." She hesitated as if she wanted to say more, but then turned and made her way to her room. I sat and listened, hearing her move around preparing for bed. When she had settled I relaxed and made up my sofa bed. I debated on sleeping clothed, and decided this first night it was the best option so my boots were the only thing removed before I lay down. Reana's scent clouded around me when I relaxed my head back into the pillow she had provided. I knew that sleep would not come easily tonight.

The sound of Reana moving about her room woke me from the light sleep I had finally drifted into the next morning. I lay there as she talked to herself and smiled. Her fox must be just as stubborn and bull headed as mine, one more reason I believed that Fate made a perfect choice for my second chance. I lay still and listened, eyes closed, as she tip toed down the hall the three steps to her bathroom. Once the door was shut I opened my eyes, and when the shower turned on I rose, folded the blanket, and decided breakfast was in order. Noting that her cupboards were bare I ran to the market just up the street while she showered.

Coffee, bacon, and eggs were prepared when Reana had finished getting ready and joined me. I smiled in greeting as she sat.

"Oh wow, Sterling, you didn't have to do this." She took a bite of bacon, moaning in appreciation. "But I do thank you. So what's on today's agenda, before I go into work, of course." She watched me as she ate, waiting.

Watching her mouth work put me in a stupor, my imagination running away with all the things I'd love for that mouth to be doing besides eating breakfast. She cleared her throat and broke the train of thought I had been going down. "Well, since I'm actively pursuing you I thought I would take you on an adventure today." I raised my coffee mug and drained the last in one gulp. "And if we happen upon friends on the way all the better."

She laughed. "You really are a sneaky devil, aren't you?"

"Not normally, but with our circumstances I have to keep you safe while planning the demise of your Alpha. Deviousness is the name of the game." I cleared her plate, washed it, and set it to dry on the counter. "I also need to keep you as far away from Wyatt and the others today as they implement their parts of our plan."

"Will you share that plan with me?" she asked as she tied the laces on her tennis shoes.

"Of course, as I told you before, I won't hide anything from you." I opened the door and waited for her. "Ready?"

She grabbed her purse and smiled. "If you are."

We made our way downstairs and she asked, "So how are we getting around if Wyatt isn't going to be with us? It's against the routine to not have a trusted driver."

"Don't worry, I have the ok to woo you unescorted." I opened the outside door to find the Ducati waiting at the curb. I watched Reana's reaction, her eyes going big and round in shock.

"You expect me to ride on that?" She pointed.

"I'll go slowly, I promise." I handed her the helmet that had been sitting on the seat.

"Where's your helmet?" she asked, not taking the one I held for her.

"I've been riding over fifty years, been in a few accidents, and still I stand. I've become a smarter driver over time, and with our quick reflexes haven't wrecked in over thirty of those years." I stepped over and placed the helmet on her, tightening the chin strap, and lovingly tapped her nose. "Come on, you'll love it."

She heaved a big sigh, adjusted her purse strap across her body, and followed. Fox and I couldn't wait to get her on the back of the bike, her body laid against ours, her arms wrapped around our waist, a connection that went further than the sexual excitement it brought. Riding with our mate would be more, so much more.

CHAPTER 16

REANA

I AM ON THE *back of a bike. How the hell did I get here?* Simple, Sterling asked and I said yes. It was becoming harder to say no to him with each passing day. I fully expected him to try and worm his way into my bed last night and he didn't. That he respected my boundaries and slept on my piece of crap couch only weakened the walls I have spent years building around my heart.

Nowhere I sit behind him on this cycle of death, my arms wrapped around him tight analyzing how he has acted over the past few days, and trying to keep my mind from all the ways we could die getting from point A to point B.

The further away from town we went the fewer cars we encountered. Soon the terrain changed from buildings and streets to wild uncharted land. Sterling slowed and took a dirt road off the main highway speeding faster than I was comfortable with. His confidence on the bike was a skill to be admired. It was as if he and the bike were one, he led and it followed like water down a riverbed. We rode for a few more miles before he slowed near a cabin. He drove around back and parked under a tree in the field behind it.

Leaning forward he motioned for me to get off first. He settled the bike on its kickstand and dismounted taking a deep breath of air into his lungs. His mouth opened to speak just as his phone rang. He fished it out of his pocket. "Damn, I need to take this. Give me a minute."

"Hello." He answered in a clipped tone. "No, not yet. Things are a little more complicated down here than what we had anticipated. Is everything ok back there?" He began to pace.

"Well, then handle it. There are always growing pains when you add new people." His face scrunched up in response to whatever the person on the other end was saying.

"Marla, I don't have time for petty squabbles." My ears perked up at his use of another female's name. "Yes, I know moving into a new place with the kids is stressful, but you can handle it. I wouldn't have left things the way I did if I didn't think you could." His eyes met mine, and by the response in his eyes he didn't like what he saw on my face.

I was not getting involved with a shifter that already had kids. I knew I shouldn't have trusted him, no matter what my flippin' hormones said. This was exactly why, he had a woman waiting for him back home. He had left her to handle moving with kids, what kind of guy does that? *Boy, you can pick em can't you, Rea, this is why we stay single, little miss foxy.*

"Change their schedules and put your foot down. You don't need me for that, now I have something more important waiting for me." He nodded as if the woman on the phone could see him. "If anything else comes up text me please." He ended the call and stepped toward me.

I stepped back. "I think I want to go home. Coming here with you wasn't a good idea."

His face registered shock, and then understanding. "Because of that call?"

"No, I just don't think this was a good idea."

"Let me explain."

"No need, just take me home please. I'll help you and your friends, we can pretend you tried to woo me. I'll even play along until your plan is done. That's it, then we don't have to see each other again."

"No" He crossed his arms over his broad chest.

"Yes." I widened my stance and mirrored his arms.

"No."

I let out a sigh. "We can stand here like this all day going back and forth but I don't feel like wasting my time. If you won't take me back I'll walk." I adjusted the strap on my purse, and was thankful I had worn sensible shoes as I started in the direction of the cabin.

"Marla works for me," Sterling started. I kept walking.

"I left her in charge of my bar back home, along with four new employees that started the day I left." He fell into step next to me. "On top of that, she is moving out of the apartment above the bar into a home that our Alpha had built for her and the two cubs she has adopted. Today she hit her limit with the bickering, and needed to let off steam and be reminded that she's strong enough to handle the responsibility I left her." He touched my arm gently, stopping my forward momentum. He waited until I raised my eyes to his. "She is a dear friend, but that's all. I am not interested in her as a female, and she is no threat to what we have."

"We don't have anything, and I absolutely do not feel threatened by her," I huffed. *Liar liar, pants on fire,* my fox chanted in my head. Ok, fine, I was pissed, but I wasn't going to admit that to him. And I was hurt, when he spoke her name he may as well twisted a knife in my heart with his own hands.

He caressed the back of his hand down the side of my face, and I fought the urge to lean into him. "My little Rea, how wrong you are, we have more than something together. Please come back and sit with me. I brought you out here away from prying ears, away from the stress, to get to know you better."

"I thought you were going to share your plan with me?"

"That too. Please." He turned and offered his arm to me. I looked from his arm to the house and back deciding I wouldn't get far on my own and I hadn't paid close enough attention to how we got here to get myself back, even if I could make it.

I turned on my heel and walked back to the tree, hearing him chuckle and fall into step behind me. His boots making shush sounds with each step. He paused at the bike, getting something from one of the saddlebags. He spread the blanket in his hands on the ground in the shade of the tree and placed a small thermal bag on it.

"Would you join me?" He gestured and opened the bag withdrawing two bottles of water and a bag of grapes.

I sat leaving plenty of room between us, taking the bottle of water he handed me only because my thirst wouldn't allow me to refuse. He leaned against the tree and watched as I drank. I wiped my mouth. "So, what's the plan, big guy?" I expected a smart response, or another attempt to get lovey dovey. Instead he turned serious and proceeded to let me know what he had discovered while I slept.

With each piece of information he shared the more dangerous I realized this pack had become, and how lucky I was that this group had showed up. The witch that had joined them did verify the spell was used on ingredients in the food. She had narrowed it down to three possible herbs, and she and the other coven members already had a spell created to counteract its damage. They were currently working on making a batch big enough for three meals. She had also found a way for the counter spell to be effectively airborne.

"Casey, Mack, and Rook will handle the

black witch that has her talons in Ricky. Talia and her coven friends are ready with a binding circle, where she will be judged and sentenced by the high witch of the Southern covens." Sterling was ticking off his fingers as he shared information.

"What about the vampires that are under her spell, they don't eat food. Will the airborne spell work on them?"

"Most likely not, as vampires don't need to breathe air either. Draven has already been working on that aspect. I don't know all the details other than it's dangerous as he is essentially replacing the tainted blood in each vampire with his own. Talia offered to help him with a regeneration spell so he could replenish his blood faster, but he politely refused. Instead he has brought in blood donors from his other nests that we know are spell free to provide his nourishment. He has assured us that the vampire guards will be spell free by the time you arrive for work tonight."

"Crap, speaking of work I need to get ready. Dammit." I stood and brushed bits of grass and dirt off my pants. "Well come on, what are you waiting for?"

"I thought you wanted to know the whole plan. I'm not finished." He smirked.

STERLING

"Let me see, the food was spelled. Your witch has a counter spell we have to put into the food for the next three meals, she also created a perfume for me to wear that releases the counter spell into the air reaching anyone near me. Draven is handling the whole tainted blood thing in ways I don't want to dwell on. Your Alpha friends will grab evil witch bitch when her spell is broken, and the local head honcho witch will judge her and put her down. This will allow someone who deserves to be Alpha to take out Ricky and we all get to live a happy existence again." I looked down at him "Did I miss anything?"

"Just the part where we can continue our mating ritual when everything is done." He stood and meticulously folded the blanket and then offered his arm. "Your chariot awaits, my lady."

I avoided his comment about mating and took his arm. "Home, James," I instructed sticking my nose in the air and acting like I envisioned some spoiled rich heiress would. I couldn't pull it off though, a bout of giggles bubbled out. This adventure had turned out better than I anticipated. I learned a lot about Sterling as we talked and he shared the plans to fix our pack. These shifters were his family, and when they found injustice or

MIRANDA LYNN

unfair handling in any pack they stepped in. They all believed in equality and unity for survival. He was fiercely loyal, and I knew he would love to a fault. *Told you, our mate, he's good.* I ignored my fox, admitting she was right about anything would only make her sassiness worse.

I snuggled up behind Sterling, helmet on, purse secured, arms wrapped tight around the man that was slowly digging his hooks into my heart. I lay my head against his back and closed my eyes. Choosing to experience the ride home through my other senses, and wanting to enjoy being so close to him while I could. Our potential future, whatever that may be, hinged on the next twenty-four hours, and the plans he and his friends had already set into play.

My main job was to act as if it was life as normal, and not let on to anything happening behind the scenes. We pulled up to my building and he shut off the bike, helped me off and guided me to the front doors with his hand on the small of my back. I was so focused on the gooseflesh his touch brought that I didn't realize one of the guards had stepped in front of us.

Sterling pulled me behind him as the guard approached. His defenses ready.

"Pardon me, sir, a package arrived from my sire, and I placed it inside the apartment on the entry table. It is clean, as are we." Sterling took a deep whiff and blew out relieved breath.

"That's good, and the others?" Sterling inquired.

"All clean and safe here and at the entrance of the club, beyond that I do not know."

"Thank you." Sterling wrapped his arm completely around my waist this time as we entered the door and ascended the stairs. By the first landing I stopped. "You have got to let me go, trying to walk up these stairs side by side while you have half your body wrapped around me is playing havoc with the little bit of balance that I have."

Sterling let out a guffaw of a laugh. "I'm sorry, Rea, it's hard to not touch you, and it's the only thing keeping my fox in check right now. He's going insane and doesn't care the reason we haven't mated yet. He doesn't have the patience or reasoning my human side does. Touching you is keeping him somewhat calm. I'm sorry." For the first time I saw the big guy blush.

"Oh." What else could I say, he had been completely honest with me and he didn't have to be. "Well then, can we hold hands? It will be easier to maneuver up the next two flights that way."

He cocked his head for a moment, and for the first time I could tell he was talking to his fox. I wondered if that was how I looked when my hussy and I spoke. His eyes came back to mine. "Yes, that will be wonderful." He laced his fingers through mine and leaned down whispering, "Thank you for understanding."

I blushed, my body leaning into his. His lips brushed my forehead sending bolts of excitement awakening parts of my body that needed to stay dormant for both our sakes. I knew that once I gave into that urge, that primal need, I would never come back to me. I admitted to myself in that moment that the loss of myself to a mate was my biggest fear.

"Let's go, little one." Sterling led the way to my apartment. I followed in a daze trying to work out how I could keep my sense of self while being his mate. I didn't think there was anyway to do both, and it hurt my soul when I decided that if I had to choose between being me or losing myself to be with my mate, I chose me. Tears filled my eyes and my fox whined at me. My heart constricted at the thought and I could already feel the crippling ache creep up my spine when I imagined a future without Sterling.

CHAPTER 17

STERLING

SAM WAS WAITING for us when we arrived that night. My suspicions were raised to see him standing outside as we pulled up.

"He's with us." Wyatt spoke before I opened the door. "He's our way in to the kitchens. Miguel had a good chat with him last night, and when he realized what we were doing he wanted to help. He's ready for a change as well. You can trust him."

I valued Wyatt's words, but the suspicion was still there. I held my hand out to Reana. "Let me have the salts, I'll deal with Sam while you go about your normal routine. The less suspicion we bring to you the better." She handed them over willingly. I could tell she was nervous about the coming evening, and the less she was involved in the implementation of our plan the better.

Reana greeted the guards as we approached and entered the club descending the stairs out of our sight. I looked at Sam, keeping my face neutral until I knew if he truly was on our side.

"Evening, Sterling! Ricky wanted me to make sure you guys made it in ok, he's heard some rumors that things are going to get sticky tonight," Sam greeted, glancing to the vamps guarding the door.

"Thanks, Sam, shall we go in?" I knew at the moment the guards that should have been on our side, weren't. I wondered what else was off the plan rail. I followed Sam down the stairs and to the left instead of right where the kitchen and dining room were. I bit my tongue, sure there were ears listening that weren't safe. Sam led me to a door that had Janitor written on it. He motioned for me to follow and I entered closing the door behind me and wincing at the loud whirring of the machinery inside. Sam grabbed a clipboard hanging on the wall and scribbled out a message.

The guards are still under Ricky's control. It's not safe to talk anywhere tonight, let your people know. Did you bring it?

He handed the board and pen to me, I read the message, nodded, and wrote a response.

Anything else I need to relay? Will you still be able to switch out the salts? Make sure to let Reana know, too. Keep her close to the bar tonight, as much as you can without raising flags.

I handed it back for him to read. A quick nod and quickly scribbled response stating that's the only change he knew of ended our non-verbal communication. He ripped the page off the pad and stuck it in his pocket. I handed over the salts and he left the room. I waited a few moments before following. At this point I had to cut off any communication with Sam for the night, and pray that he followed through with protecting Reana as best he could.

I opened the pack bond and let everyone know that the vamps were compromised and not clean. *Change in plans, the vamps aren't trustworthy. Beware.*

Relishing the quiet of the hallway after being bombarded by sounds in the Janitor's room was a relief. My phone pinged with an incoming message. I swiped it open.

More back-up has been sent and should be waiting for you. Mack and Casey have brought them up to date on plans. Ricky is suspicious so this needs to go down tonight. Rook and Jazz will join you as well. Best of luck and report back when you can. —J

"Who the hell has he sent now?" I wondered out loud. I entered the club, head still down, and ran smack dab into the newest addition to our team. I smiled, recognizing his scent. Having a bear on our side was a good choice.

"Sorry, boss, I didn't know you were coming in. Rook told me to come find you." Barrett stepped back.

I grinned at all six foot six of him. "So you're the backup." I reached out to shake his hand, welcoming the added muscle. "Glad to have you man, and perfect timing. You must have done something to impress Jerome to be sent on such an important trip so early into your membership." I inclined my head toward the bar, inviting him to sit with me.

"I guess." He shrugged his wide, flannel covered shoulders. "When the Alpha asks for your help you go, no matter where you are."

Sam placed two mugs of coffee in front of us and disappeared again. "Rook has you all set up?" I had to be careful what words I used, ears were everywhere, and many were untrusted.

"Yes, sir. I'm here to help protect your interest until you depart." Barrett knew the game, and took a long gulp of coffee as he turned to watch the waitresses prepare for the crowd building outside. "You have business to attend to tonight, so I will ensure that she is safe and untouched." His eyes followed Reana as she bustled about.

Ricky descended the stairs. "I didn't know you were bringing more friends, Sterling." He wasn't happy and made it obvious.

"We need to discuss some things, and I want to make sure that Reana stays untouched while I am unavailable. You do remember that while I'm here I have permission to pursue her?"

"Of course, but a bodyguard isn't needed. Everyone has been notified she's off limits," he huffed.

"Your pack yes, but other patrons that come and go from this club haven't been and aren't under your jurisdiction. She will not be touched by anyone, and Barrett here," I slapped him on the shoulder, "is going to see to that for me." I smiled, and Barrett glared down at Ricky, face stern, allowing his bear to rise and fall behind his eyes.

"Whatever. I still don't see why it was necessary." He averted his eyes, fidgeting. "Shall we begin?" Ricky was extremely antsy tonight. The fear wafted off him in thick waves, it was almost visible. The stench clogged my nose and made my eyes water. His skin was paler than normal as well, accenting the hollows in his cheeks and dark circles under his eyes. His pores seemed to seep a tar-like substance that coated his skin like oil floating on water.

"Lead the way. Let's get this over with so I can enjoy my evening." I followed Ricky up the two flights of stairs to his office. Fox was not happy, and was doing his best to stop me from going on, his hackles raised as he growled at me. I couldn't just stop so I opened my senses and sent out a quick, *"Be Alert,"* through the bond. I should have heeded that warning myself. I crossed the threshold into his office and felt the slime of magic fall and coat me, cutting off all mental communication, including that of my fox. My body felt heavy, and I could hardly move.

"My dear cunning fox, you think to beat me in my own game?"

I glanced to my left, my eyes the only thing that could move, and saw her emerge from the shadows cloaked in a thick velvet hooded robe. Her voice wove magic through the air as she walked, it radiated off her in waves of grey and black. She didn't walk as much as float across the floor until she hovered in front of me.

"Your little band of merry men and sweet little witch are no match for me. I will enjoy tearing them apart, one by one." She leaned in and caressed my face, her nails digging small valleys along my jaw. I had no control over my body, frozen in place and at her mercy. She withdrew and licked the droplets of blood from her long pointed nails. "I am pleased to see little Casey here too, I have unfinished business with her. Come join me at the window, I want you to watch, to see that no one can defeat me, my power is too strong."

My legs moved jerkily as her magic acted as a remote control. My body moved against my will taking me to look out over the club.

"Richard, get our guest a chair. He'll need to sit for our demonstration." She snapped her fingers and he ran to do her bidding. "You see, Sterling, I had planned to take your dear Reana first, but had a change of heart. She will be my last victim. I want to enjoy her torment and savor your destruction having to watch unable to help her."

"Is there anything else I can assist you with, Maura?"

She hissed at him, whipping around and pinning him with her red gaze. "I have told you one too many times to never use my name. Names have power, or have you not learned that lesson, Richard?" She made a twisting motion with her fingers, since he was behind me I couldn't tell what she was doing, but by the grunts he let out I assumed she immobilized him.

"Now, let's get back to tonight's entertainment. I will deal with your transgression later, Richard." She adjusted the ends of her sleeves and dusted invisible lint from them.

I could do nothing but glance between her and the window and wait. To see what she planned and how she would do it. I continued to try and contact my pack members, now that I knew her name I needed to get that information to someone. She was right, in the magical realm names had immense power.

"Ah, there she is. Your sweet Reana, she really is a hard worker, and excellent at her job. I do hate to lose good employees." She sighed as if it was a big decision she was making. "Hmm who shall we make first on our list?" She hummed as she carefully scanned the growing crowd, "Ah yes, he'll do nicely." She chanted under her breath and extended one pointy nailed, gnarled finger releasing a thin stream of black oily smoke. I followed the path as it wove through the crowd toward its target realizing at the last minute she had chosen Barrett. The smoke floated around his head swirling down to his nose. He took a breath and the smoked shot up, making him sneeze and cough. He recovered from the small fit and shook his head as if to clear his mind. "Wonderful, now let's have some fun. My dear bear, show us how ferocious you can be, will you. It's time the dragon met his match." She glanced at me with a twinkle in her red eye. "Yes, I know all your secrets, dear fox, let's see who wins this match."

Barrett started moving forward and then stopped. Shaking his head and sneezing again.

"Yes, find the dragon," she whispered, pushing a bit more magic into her words.

Barrett began to move again, but stopped and turned his head toward the bar. Sam was waving him back with a fresh drink and a plate of food. Reana passed him at that same moment and whatever hold the witch's words had on him were broken. Barrett turned and sat back down on the stool he had occupied moments before tearing into his sandwich and guzzling the beer Sam had placed on the bar. The weight of magic in the room thickened.

"No, that's not possible," Maura whispered and quickly chanted sending another tendril of magical smoke directly at Barrett. This one met with resistance as it reached him, it snaked around trying to find a crack in the barrier that seemed to be surrounding him now. "Impossible!" Maura growled. She threw the hood of her cloak back revealing her dark stringy hair and turned her blazing gaze upon me. "You, explain!"

I felt the magic that had held my tongue immobile release. I coughed and smiled at her. "Looks like you don't know all our tricks."

She slapped me, her nails scraping new trails across my cheek. "Tell me." She put more magical force behind her words. I was thankful Talia had given us her counter spell. It didn't help me with the hold Maura had on my body, or how she had shut off the mental connections I had, but it did allow me to fight the compulsion Maura was trying to push on me to tell our plans. "You can try all you want, but I won't tell you how. Maura, tonight will be your last night of control. You will see as the night progresses that your powers will lose, bit by bit. Your reign is over."

"NOOO, you are wrong. My powers are stronger than hers, your little white witch is no match for me." She swelled up, her power filling the room, the windows beginning to moan with the pressure. She focused on growing and pulling power into her that her hold on my mind slipped, just a bit, but enough for a connection to come through.

Sterling, where are you? What the hell is going on? I recognized Rook's voice. Not knowing how long the connection would stay I chose my words carefully.

Her name is Maura, use it, she's going to attack any moment. BE READY.

The connection snapped liked an overstretched rubber band, making my head pound in pain that radiated down my spine and spread to every nerve.

"Nice try, fox, for that you will pay and so will your beloved mate." Maura focused her gaze and all the power she had pulled into her at the windows, shattering them and sending the pieces into the crowd. The smoke that had been gathering at her feet snaked over the window ledge and down into the crowd, tendrils searching for those she wished to destroy. The club goers cheered, thinking this a part of tonight's show.

Wyatt and Miguel started to evacuate as

many people as possible, but found it difficult to get people to listen. Everyone was glued to the window waiting for the next part of the show. Finally someone hit the fire alarm setting off the strobing red lights and alarm spurring the crowd into a frenzy.

Maura floated through the shattered window arms outstretched and eyes glowing bright. Her fingers twisted throwing spells as she went. The club doors slammed shut, trapping those left inside as she landed on the dance floor softly, surrounded by the oily tendrils of black magic she controlled. Six robed figures appeared from different points in the club and approached her, placing themselves evenly spread in a circle around her. The smoke at her feet disappeared and I was freed from the magical bonds tying me to the chair. I leapt through the window landing on the first floor with a tuck and roll move learned years ago during my brief obsession with becoming a stunt man. I sniffed once and let my nose guide me to where Reana was hiding, Sam next to her, and Barrett fighting off anyone who came near. I skidded to a halt at the half shifted state I found Barrett in. He was new to the pack, and I hadn't had the chance to see him in his shifted state, let alone partially shifted as he was. I didn't know if he'd recognize me or if his animal would be in full control.

I approached slowly, hands raised. "Barrett, man, you good?"

His eyes turned to me, his mouth no longer a mouth but the snout of his bear, his arms and shoulders his bear forelegs, and his hands giant mauling paws of his bear. But his eyes were those of his human side. He chuffed through his snout and winked. That's all I needed, I squeezed behind him and squatted down to check on Reana. I swept her into my arms, hugging her to me. "I was so worried, are you okay, did any of the glass get you?" I leaned back enough to scan her and confirm she was ok.

"No, I'm okay. I'm not hurt. Barrett grabbed me when the window shattered and pushed me back here, Sam came and stayed with me. We are ok. What about you?" She ran her hands over my face, lightly touching the scrapes and scratches I had forgotten were there. "I couldn't find you anywhere and you didn't come when I called." Tears began to fill her eyes. "I thought you had left, or worse, were dead."

I pulled her to me again, nestling her head in my shoulder, and caressed her hair in comfort. Placing small kisses anywhere I could. "No, I didn't leave you. These are just superficial, and will be healed before we even leave. She captured me as I walked into Ricky's office cutting off all my communication and immobilizing me for her entertainment. It's a long story that I'll share with everyone when this is over. Just know that I would have been there if I had heard, nothing would have kept me away."

The din of the chaos on the other side of the bar died down and left only the sound of the six robed women chanting and Maura screaming her response. "You have no power over me, this is temporary! You think to imprison me? I've escaped every prison ever developed for me."

Sam, Reana, and I stood up to watch. Reana's pack members were sitting or leaning around the room, holding their heads and looking disoriented. Maura was in the center of the dance floor, the robed witches had removed their hoods and we could now see that they each stood on a specific point of an intricately drawn circle. Each witch stood before a symbol drawn into the scrolling flow of the circle. "A containment circle," I whispered.

"Yeah, they came in early this morning to draw it, and then spelled it to look like the regular floor," Sam added. "It was only revealed once she descended as her feet touched the dance floor."

"It won't hold her long," I predicted just as a very tall white cloaked individual emerged from the darkness behind Maura.

"You are correct, fox." Her voice boomed through the room as she lowered the hood. Maura paled and turned toward her. "Hello Maura, it's so good to finally catch up with you." Her voice continued to carry around the club.

"No, you died. I saw you die," Maura whispered her stature shrinking with the words.

"Oh dear child, you know that I cannot die. As long as magic carries on so shall I, but you, dear girl, have outlived her due. You have taken the gifts the goddess gave you and twisted them into something evil, dark, and destructive. You have used them for self-gain, revenge, and have become drunk on the power. You had so much potential, and I had such high hopes for you. It saddens me to have to come here and dole out the justice that I must." Her sadness blanketed us, all her emotions pure and true.

"Your powers can't touch me. You have no say over what I do now." Maura tried to bolster herself.

"This is true, my power cannot touch you,

but not for the reasons you think. You have taken on the evil slime that blood magic leaves behind, and that evil is a contaminant that I cannot let infect the pureness of magic that I represent. But there is one here who has the magic and power that can finally help lay you to rest peacefully." The grand witch raised her eyes and searched the room until they landed on Wyatt. "If he is willing to help us." She gestured for him to come forward. "My dear dragon, I would never assume to command how you use your amazing gift and talents. But I do implore you to help me. I do not want to drag out Maura's life in a prison, chained from her life essence, so I ask if you would be so gracious as to help remove her and the taint she has left on this pack. I ask that you release her life essence from this world so that I may help guide it on to the next." She bowed to him.

I knew that Wyatt's animal was a dragon, but he never shared much of what he could do, and I had never seen him transform before. Dragons were few and far between, and all that is known of them now is simply stories passed down that have turned into a types of fairy tale. I was curious to see how this would play out.

"Wyatt's a dragon?" Reana whispered in

awe.

"Yes, little fox, that he is, and one from the oldest line known to the magical world," the priestess replied. "There is no need to be scared, any of you. He is a shifter to be respected and treasured by those he considers friends and family." She smiled at him. "He is friend to shifters and witches alike. He bridges the gap between us."

Wyatt kneeled before the priestess bowing his head. "It would be my honor to assist the goddess in any way that I can."

"Goddess?" Reana turned to me. I shrugged my shoulders. I didn't know either.

"I thought she was a high priestess," Sam added.

The goddess answered our questions. "The priestess and I are close, and for this event she welcomed me in. My true form would not fit in this building, and would overwhelm you all, destroying who you truly are. In this realm I can only manifest when a true follower, pure of heart, opens themselves and allows me to reside within them. I cannot stay in this form long or I will do damage that will be irreparable to my dear priestess." She turned to Wyatt. "If you will assist me now I would like to return home and take my dear daughter Maura's essence with me."

Wyatt shimmered before us, growing and expanding into a glorious beast. People moved away giving him room. His form grew to a height that towered above the second floor of the club, though his body only expanded to the room vacated by the patrons. He looked oddly like a giraffe and Reana giggled next to me. Wyatt turned his head toward us, his silver eyes glowing with mirth as smoke trailed from his nose.

Not everyone was as calm about seeing a dragon. The goddess raised her arms and addressed the crowd. "There is no reason to fear our friend Wyatt, he is only here to help. His fire is the only magic that can release Maura from the evil she has welcomed in. His breath will burn the residue left by her ministrations allowing her body to be sent back to the earth and her essence to leave with me to rest for eternity." She rested a hand on his scaled foreleg. "If his fire reaches anyone else it will simply flow over you and feel like a warm hug."

Reana leaned into me. "Do you see their faces? No one believes her, and I don't blame them. We are being asked to believe that a goddess walks in the skin of this priestess, and that a huge scary dragon isn't going to burn us all alive."

I chuckled, knowing both Wyatt and the priestess would have heard her. Wyatt proved me right when he wrapped his tail around her waist moments later as the goddess addressed us all.

"I see many of you still don't believe, so I ask that our dear Reana come forward and let us demonstrate that his fire will hurt no one that he doesn't intend it to."

Reana stared at me, and I nodded my encouragement for her to go forward. "You know Wyatt would never hurt you, show everyone that you trust him and they will follow."

She scowled and turned to Wyatt. "If you singe one hair on my head I'm going to beat you when you transform back. Why do I have to be the demonstration?" She stomped forward and then stopped pointing to Maura. "You've got her, right? She can't get out or send any slimy spells my way?"

My eyes followed her as Reana took her place. "Our mate is brave," Fox said with pride. "How are you so sure that she is our mate? You and I both know we aren't worthy of her. The Fates must have made a mistake." I knew what my instincts told me, but my human side still held strong to the fact that I didn't deserve another mate. I couldn't protect my last one, how could I truly protect Reana?"We have changed much over the years, learned, grown, and we have more friends now who can help us." Fox was persistent. "She doesn't deserve us, she is worthy of someone much better." I wanted Reana to be happy and secure. Security wasn't something we could give her, not with the threats still looming beyond this room. "Stop, we are good enough, and we will protect her. She is OURS!" Fox sat on his haunches and huffed at me, ending our internal conversation. That was his signal that he wouldn't budge, and my human side usually caved to his wisdom. This time would be no different.

The goddess waved her hands and revealed that the chants the circle of witches were speaking actually wove themselves into magical chains that wrapped around Maura and cloaked her in a golden cage. "Does that calm your mind?" she teased.

"Yes, thank you." Reana nodded in affirmation and continued to just outside the circle. "Okay, what do I do now?"

"Simply stand there and allow Wyatt's fire to flow," the goddess instructed.

Wyatt lowered his head until his chin was almost on the floor and his eyes could meet Reana's, then he blew a small stream of fire that began at her feet and wrapped around her until she was fully encased in flame, but not on fire. Everyone watched as she raised her arm and looked at the fire dancing along her skin. Then her face split into the biggest smile I had ever seen on her face.

"Wyatt, this is amazing. It feels so warm and cozy, and I feel safe and oddly loved." Rea giggled. "How long will it last?"

Wyatt answered by snuffing against her hair and the flames died out. She hugged his snout without thought, and he leaned his dragon head into her embrace smiling only as a dragon could.

"Thank you, my child." The goddess looked on with loving eyes as Reana came back to stand with me. She wrapped her arms around me and squeezed.

"That was so cool." She smiled. "I want to do it again." Her attention was grabbed by the scene unfolding on the dance floor. The circle glowed brighter as Wyatt began to direct his fire down to Maura.

I didn't know what to expect, screaming obscenities, the scent of burning flesh, or worse. Instead, we watched as the darkness was swallowed by the dragon fire and Maura became a younger version of herself. We watched time reverse before our eyes, until she was a young white witch. She smiled as tears streamed down her face. "Thank you, I am so tired and ready to rest." She stared at the goddess as Wyatt's fire continued to swallow her magic.

Moments later Maura's body lay prone on the floor and the goddess held a small ball of light in her hands. She turned to Wyatt "Thank you, my dragon friend, for your assistance. I am sure we all here will agree to keep your secret, those that can't will have the experience removed from their memories." She waved her empty hand in an arc, and the magic she spread settled down on us all.

Wyatt's massive form began to shrink has he shifted into his human form. He bowed to the goddess and joined Reana, Sam, and I at the bar. Reana hugged him tight. I met Wyatt's eyes over her head and promised with a look to wipe the smug smile off his face if he did anything inappropriate. Wyatt laughed out loud at my face.

"What did I miss?" Reana asked looking between us.

I wrapped my arm around her shoulders bringing her back to my side and kissed her head. "Nothing, my little fox."

"I must leave you all now, thank you for your help, and blessings to you all." The goddess departed the priestess's body in a large glowing orb, we could see the smaller circle that represented Maura's essence encased inside as she rose and passed through the ceiling.

Everyone began moving about and the rest of our team joined us to wait for the crowd to leave. The threat was gone, the pack was safe again, and it was time to address the bond between my little fox and myself.

CHAPTER 18

REANA

STERLING WHISKED ME out of the club shortly after the confrontation had ended. Sam promised he would make sure that Suzy got home safely. Things were still in an upheaval, and I worried about my other pack mates who were simply victims of Ricky and his witch bitch.

The fear that gripped me rose up again as the scene from tonight played back in my mind as we traveled the short distance home. Sterling had said he would always come when I called him, but as I watched him follow Ricky up the stairs my heart clenched with fear. My fox wanted to chase after him, the hairs along her back raised in defense. She sensed something I couldn't. I ignored the urge and went to work, constantly glancing at the balcony waiting to see Sterling standing there but he never showed. Time seemed to slow as I watched the window in Ricky's office explode outward, shards of glass raining down on the dance floor below.

Barrett grabbed me and shoved me behind the bar blocking my view of what happened next. The screams of the patrons and the haze of black smoke ratcheted up my fear. I just knew then that Sterling was dead, he had to be. I had cried for him, yelled for him, and he never came. He had promised he would always come and he hadn't.

The SUV stopped and jerked me out of my memories. Not a word was exchanged as Sterling and I climbed the stairs to my apartment. He unlocked and did his normal security search before letting me in. I could tell by the look on his face that he wanted to talk, but I wasn't ready. I headed straight for the shower when we arrived, I needed to scrub off the last feeling of ickiness.

I donned my favorite pair of pajama pants and t-shirt and stared at myself in the mirror. So much had happened over the past few days. My fox sashayed to look through my eyes. *"Quit stalling, mate is waiting."* She impatiently yipped in my head. *"It's too soon, I can't mate with anyone right now. What about the pack and the changes? Where do we fit with it all? I'm scared."* I touched my face, taking note of each little line and the dark circles under my eyes. For the first time in years I could relax and not worry if I would live until tomorrow.

"Mating happens on the Fates schedule, not yours. He is OUR mate. Protecter, lover, friend. He is everything." Damn she was a huffy little bitch when it came to something she wanted. *"Trust your instincts, trust me. The Fates would never hurt us."*

She was right, if I didn't take the chance I would never know. It was time to stop being scared and take charge of my life. I smiled at my reflection and left the bathroom drying the ends of my hair with my towel to find Sterling relaxed on my couch sans shirt. My mouth went dry. He was tapping furiously on his phone and seemed oblivious to my entrance. I stood there appreciating the slight movement of muscle along his back as he worked his phone.

"Did the shower help, my little fox?"

So much for him not knowing I was there. I, of course would be able to detect every move I made. "Yes, I feel much better. Is everything ok?" I settled on the opposite end of the couch from him.

"Yes, I was just touching base with Wyatt and Mack. They rounded up Ricky and his cronies, and have detained them to ensure the spell is broken. The shifter council called an emergency meeting and unanimously agreed on their sentence. Once the local coven declares them free of the black magic they will be flown to London. There they will be collared and imprisoned for life or until the council decides they have served time. Mack and Rook will help the pack regroup and develop a new hierarchy. The club is closed until further notice."

"So Ricky won't be the Alpha? If he isn't, who will be? And what do you mean by 'they will be collared?'"

"That's part of what Rook and Mack will help ascertain. Casey is headed back to her pride with Jasmine on one of Leo's jets. The cubs need her, and the pride needs Jasmine right now. The collaring is one of the harshest punishments for shifters. The collar is magically spelled to prevent them from shifting. They will serve their time in human form. But enough about pack business, I think we have better things to talk about." He rested his arm on the back of the couch as he looked at me straight on. "Fox won't let me put off talking about the mating pull between us."

I held my breath. I had hoped we would have more time before that subject came up, but my own fox was chattering away at me, hiking her ass up in offering. Sterling's gaze set off tingles along my spine, and the longer he gazed at me the more intense they got. "What about it?" I tried to blow it off.

"Steven isn't here, and hasn't been around the past day, I'm holding on to my need by a thread. I know you have been through a lot, but I can't keep fox at bay. We need to know if you will accept us as mate, if we have a chance, or not." He leaned forward, elbows on knees, and breathed deeply. "You know about my past, and that you aren't my first mate. You also know it's rare for a shifter to have more than one in a lifetime. I've argued with my fox, I never thought I was worthy of a second chance, but he insists that Fate has different plans. At this point I have to believe and follow my feelings." He raised his eyes to me again. "She has chosen, fox has chosen, but do you choose?"

The raw emotion I saw in his eyes broke down another wall around my heart, the pieces shattering into the wind. The emotions and feelings this man evoked threw me for a hell of a ride, and it scared me. But filtering through it all at the core was safety, a sense of home, and the sexual connection was sizzling. The fact that he had restrained himself for this long was a miracle, and showed the respect he had for me as a woman as well as a female shifter. These days it was rare to find a mate of the same species.

"Things have happened so fast over the past few days, I admit that my fox agrees. She has chosen you, I have lived a long life under the fear that there wasn't a mate out there for me. Facing the realization that you sit here in my living room, I want to run away screaming and jump your bones at the same time." I broke the connection of his gaze and stared at the twisted towel in my hands, an outward sign of my nerves.

The couch dipped as he scooted closer. His hand closed over both of mine, stopping the twisting motion. "I am grateful for your honesty. Let me assure you that I would never hurt you. I would always put your safety and protection above all others, even my own. But I won't lock you away, I won't prohibit you from doing anything you choose, as long as it doesn't bring harm to yourself or others. Reana, as a mate you would be cherished, loved, and respected. I also hope to bring joy, laughter, and a lightness to your life. If you give us the chance."

His scent wrapped around me whispering along my skin raising goose flesh along my arms. I raised my head, our noses were an inch apart at most, his eyes hopeful as they met mine. I couldn't speak, so I leaned forward and met his lips with mine in answer. His breath sucked in at the contact and his hands framed my face angling me for better access. His tongue ran along the seam of my lips seeking entrance and I opened willingly. I grasped his biceps feeling the muscles tensed beneath the skin. I held on as his kiss took my need higher. My core throbbed in time with my heart, my breasts ached with the need to be touched.

Sterling broke the kiss, leaning his forehead against mine. "Is that a yes, my little fox?"

I giggled awkwardly. "Yes"

"Finally," he whispered as he stood and swept me into his arms, depositing me on my bed moments later. "Too many clothes." Evidence of his excitement strained against the front of his jeans. His eyes roamed down my body, stopping when he reached my nipples, now hardened and pebbled beneath my t-shirt.

I sat forward and grabbed the hem of my shirt, divesting myself of the irritating material and allowing the cool air to caress my heated flesh. Sterling still stood there, just staring, and I began to doubt whether I should have taken my shirt off. I went to cover myself and he reached out.

"No, don't. You are just so beautiful, I have no words." He joined me on the bed crawling over me. I lay back as his lips met mine in another scorching kiss. I could get lost in just his kiss alone. He lowered his chest until we were skin to skin and my body reacted in a frenzy. I had to touch him and I did anywhere my hands would reach. I had expected things to go slow, but I couldn't wait now.

He reached down pushing at the waist of my pajama bottoms. I raised up and helped him remove them. He kissed his way down my neck, biting lightly on the spot I knew he would place his mark when he claimed me fully. He continued until his tongue found my hardened nipple, laving and twirling around it. His hand caressed the other pinching lightly and rubbing the sting away, the same as he was doing with his teeth and tongue.

I let go, allowing my body to react without thought. My emotions were swirling, and I swore I could feel his as well.

He continued down my body until he reached the wetness pooled between my thighs. I watched as he inhaled deeply before running the flat of his tongue up my most sensitive skin. His eyes met mine and he grinned before diving in. Sensations cascaded down on me and I couldn't hold my head up to watch any longer. He found a rhythm of licking and sucking that had my hips moving of their own accord and little mewling sounds escaping from my throat. It didn't take long for the tension to build, my orgasm on the brink. He chose that moment to leave, a cool burst of air invaded the space between my legs where he had just been.

My eyes popped open to see him ridding himself of the rest of his clothing and repositioning between my legs. The engorged head of his throbbing cock teased at my entrance. "I want to be inside you when you come" He growled at me. I reached up and brought him down for another kiss. "I don't know how long I'll last this time Rea, my need has been building for you for the last few days."

"I just need to feel you." My voice was raspy with emotion, and a moan of pleasure escaped as he entered me. I was tight, sex hadn't been a priority in a while, but his patience paid off, by the third stroke he was fully seated and I felt completely whole for the first time in my life.

"Rea, baby, look at me. I need your eyes on me." I did and watched his face as he stroked in and out, rotating his hips searching to see what pleased me and what didn't. He studied my face as hard as I studied his as I ran my fingers up his arms and scraped my nails down his back. That made him twitch inside me. My fingers along his neck elicited the same reaction.

Sterling's rhythm picked up and I could sense he was close, I wasn't but that was ok. I saw in his eyes the determination he had to hold out. I smiled, pulled his head down for a kiss and ran my nails down his back, hard. I felt that twitch again and decided he deserved a good release. I clenched my inner walls and within two strokes Sterling was coming hard. Yup, now that was power, I didn't care that my orgasm had fallen away, knowing that my touch set my mate off was a heady feeling indeed.

"Why did you..." Sterling breathed hard through his words.

"Because I could."

"It's my job to see to your satisfaction". He pouted as he rolled to his side facing me. "I'm sorry I let you down."

"Just stop that. You didn't let me down, have you never known a woman who experimented to see if her touch inside and out could drive you mad?"

"Honestly," he trailed his fingers own my naked chest, "no. But I think I like that idea, and consider it a challenge on my part."

I felt his eagerness grow against my thigh. "Already?"

"For you, always." He rolled me over to straddle him. "But this time your pleasure comes first."

I leaned down and licked the crevice between his neck and shoulder. "This means I get to mark you first, right?"

"My darling Reana, you can mark me anywhere you want."

"Will you mark me at the same time?" I had always dreamed my mating would be that way. It wasn't usual for the female to leave a mark on her male, but recently it had become more popular. Equaling the playing field, like a pair of wedding bands, only permanent.

"If that's what you wish."

I placed my hands on his chest and positioned myself ready to slide down his length. I lowered just until his tip touched my outer lips, and leaned forward to where I would place my mark. I let my fox out just enough for my canines to lengthen and turned slightly meeting Sterling's eyes his fox looking out at me. I smiled and bit down hearing his growl of satisfaction right before his teeth pierced my skin. His rammed into my core as our marks began to heal, completing the mating. The bond opened between us and emotions swarmed through my head like a tidal wave. Feeling both his arousal and my own sent me over the edge, tingling every nerve ending.

The bond wrapped us in a cocoon of pack magic the rest of the night. I learned that night my mate was true to his word, and always ready and willing. I finally tired to the point I couldn't move about three am and snuggled into his warmth sleep taking over instantly.

I woke up thinking my apartment must be on fire with the heat that surrounded me, but realized quickly it was just the man next to me radiating warmth that rivaled Mount Saint Helens before eruption. An arm tightened around my middle when I tried to get up bringing forth the realization that I was still completely naked and the fact that I had to pee desperately. I tried moving the offending appendage again and only seemed to encourage it to tighten further.

"Sterling, I need to use the restroom."

"Just a few more minutes," he grumbled.

"My bladder can't hold it for a few more minutes." I huffed. He moved so I could do what

I needed to. The cold air hitting me as soon as I vacated the furnace that was my bed did not help my cause. I grabbed my robe off the floor and rushed to the bathroom. I was now fully awake, thanks to a cold apartment and a block of ice for a toilet seat. I set about making a pot of coffee in my small kitchen.

Sterling entered just as the pot finished perking. He looked yummy in the morning. Rumpled hair, no shirt, and jeans still unbuttoned and riding low on his hips. I pulled another mug out of the cupboard and poured both of us our first jolt of caffeine for the day. He followed as I sat them on the small kitchen table and wrapped his arms around me, pulling me against him so he could nuzzle my hair.

"I waited for you to come back to bed, little one." He nipped his mark on my neck and sent shivers through me.

"I was too awake to go back to bed." I turned in his arms and kissed him quick. "Sorry." I disengaged from him and retrieved the sugar and creamer. I doctored my cup and looked across the table at where he sat watching me. "So now what?"

"What do you mean?" He quirked his head.

"Well, we are mated, correct? Now what?

What happens now?" I blew on my coffee before taking a sip.

"Well we decide that. It seems you have an idea already if you are asking the questions. Tell me."

"Well, one thing that confuses me. When we mated last night I was flooded with emotions and feelings that weren't mine. I heard your thoughts, and could feel the pack web to your pack, but I no longer feel mine. This morning I can still feel the new pack web, but your feelings and thoughts are gone. Why?"

"I'm sorry, Rea, I didn't realize that I still had my block in place. Last night I thought everything was a bit overwhelming so I put a mental block up to cut those off for now. I thought to talk to you about how you wanted to proceed with that part of the bond. It can be sudden and confusing, but I will never keep anything from you." He closed his eyes a moment and suddenly I could feel and hear him once again. "You let me know if it's every too much, over time you'll get used to it, and it won't be so overwhelming."

Once he had dropped the wall everything felt right again. Yes, it was weird having him in my head essentially, but my fox loved that she could now romp around with his. "It's not overwhelming, it feels right, and I feel whole. Plus, I think my fox is enjoying getting to romp with yours." I smiled and blushed a bit. "Now where do we go from here?"

I'm sure he could feel my unease at not knowing where our lives would go from here. I hadn't been in my pack for too long, but I did have friends that I wanted to make sure were ok. Beyond that I was open to going where he went. In my heart I knew home would always be where Sterling was, no matter how often we moved around.

"Don't worry, my little one, we won't move around. I would like to take you home to my family though. I think you'll love them, and I know they'll love you. I have a home and a business that I need to return to and want you by my side the whole way." He stood and refilled his mug, leaning against the counter as he continued. "As for your pack here, there is a lot of healing that needs to happen. Mack and Rook are going to help get things started, and I am sure Leo will be available for support until they get the new Alpha established." Sterling stopped but I knew there was more he was debating in his mind.

You know I can hear you here as well. I pointed to my head as I sent the message through our bond.

He smiled. "Yes, I suppose I'll have to get used to that as well, having my mate know my every thought. I want to take you back to my pack as soon as possible. We eliminated one threat, but there is still another out there, and having you on my home turf would make me feel better."

"The Resistance," I stated.

"Yes, we had to choose to fight them or the evil plaguing the pack. Of course The Resistance has gone underground again while we dispatched the most imminent threat. We don't know when or where they will pop up again. The last stretch between appearances was fifty years, but that was due to the fact we had taken out their leaders then. We didn't accomplish that this time, so I feel it won't be as long of a wait this time. The only sure thing I know is they won't show up in Texas again."

"What about the vampires?"

"Those that were working with the pack have been called back to their nest for now. Draven will oversee them for the next few months before he returns home. Whether they will work with shifters again is unknown."

"Okay. I want to see Sam and Suzy before we go. Then I'll be ready to see your home and your family." I took my mug to the sink and rinsed it out. Sterling gently turned me and framed my face with his hands.

"It's our home and our family now, mate. Best start remembering that." The kiss that followed curled my toes and weakened my knees. At this rate we wouldn't get anywhere but back to my bedroom. "That is a wonderful idea, but it will have to wait. The next time I take you will be in our bedroom." He patted my ass. "Now go get dressed so we can go say goodbye to your friends."

My phone rang as I passed it on the counter. I grabbed it and didn't recognize the number. I turned the screen toward Sterling with a raised eyebrow. His lips split into a grin.

"It's ok, go ahead and answer it."

I thumbed the answer button. "Hello."

"Hey, Reana, and I assume Sterling is standing right there with you. This is Casey, Jasmine and I are currently heading back to the pride, but we wanted to call and officially welcome you into the family. We felt the ripple along the bond when you completed your mating. We are so excited to have another girl in the family."

I smiled and Sterling rubbed circles on my lower back, his love and joy pulsing through our bond. "Thank you, I'm happy to truly be a part of a family again."

"Call me when you get settled back home and we'll have a good girls chat." Casey laughed.

"I'd like that. Very much."

"Great, well our ride is here. Sterling, all I have to say is you hurt her in anyway and I'll be on the first plane back to kick your ass. You know I can, too," Casey warned. "Again, welcome, Rea, and I'll talk to you soon." The line went silent as she hung up. I looked up at Sterling.

"She can kick your ass, huh?" I poked his chest teasing.

"She'll never need to as I don't ever plan to hurt you." I found myself wrapped in his arms and never wanting to leave.

"As much as I enjoy being wrapped in your warmth if I don't get dressed we'll never make it out of here today." I pushed against his chest and he released me walking over to pick up his shirt from the back of the couch. "I'll be back in a jiff." I hurried down the five step hallway and grabbed the first pair of jeans and shirt I found. Bra, underwear, socks, and I was ready to go.

CHAPTER 19

THE NEXT FEW hours were happy and sad at the same time. Saying goodbye to my friends didn't take long, but meeting with the members of my new pack and the hugs and welcome did. Rook and Mack were typical guys. Lovingly hugging and welcoming me, and then giving Sterling a good ribbing, lots of back slapping, and male grunting.

I sat in the apartment they used and watched, joy filled and happy. Wyatt joined me on the couch as the guys acted like guys. I looked at him. "Why aren't you joining the male bonding moment?" I smiled.

"It's their moment. I'm not part of their pack. I work with Leo, I watch his back, but don't belong to any particular pack." He looked on with a type of sadness about him.

"Wait, then how were they able to talk to you through the bonds?"

"That's a long story, but Leo and Jerome figured that out decades ago. Leo and I are the only ones outside the pack that can communicate with them. That I know of."

"Well that makes you family then." I nodded to emphasize my words as truth.

"Leo maybe, me I'm a tool, a resource they call on in times of crisis. I'm ok with that. My dragon isn't released often, but he's ready when called upon." He finally looked at me again. "Congratulations to you and Sterling. You both deserve it, and if you ever need my help you just have to call." He tapped his temple and stood to leave.

"I'll walk you out." I stood and followed him to the elevator doors. "Thank you, Wyatt." I surprised him by hugging him hard and kissing his cheek. "Travel safe, watch your back, and call me or Sterling if YOU ever need help." I tapped my temple and smiled as the elevator doors closed.

I turned to find Sterling and the rest of his crew standing there. "Leo has a jet ready to take us back whenever we want," he informed me.

"Oh, that was fast. Well, I suppose I should go pack."

"No need, Rea, we've got that covered. Steven already has a U-Haul on the way to your place with two big burly vamps loaned to us by Draven. Your apartment will be packed up and headed back to Sterling's place before you take off." Miguel clapped his hands together smiling.

"Oh, umm." I switched to the mate bond. *I'll still need my essentials, Sterling, and my laptop.*

"Already taken care of, a bag was packed and left downstairs. We'll grab it on the way out. I'm anxious to get you home, and Marla has been texting all morning wanting to know when Barrett is coming back." Sterling laughed. "The big guy is waiting downstairs for us, so say your goodbyes to these buffoons and let's go. I'm ready to get you home." His eyes flashed with heat and promises.

Rook, Mack, and Miguel enthusiastically welcomed me to the family with twirling hugs. By the time I got to Steven I felt like a James Bond martini. Shaken not stirred. Steven was more hesitant in his embrace until I wrapped my arms snug around him letting him know how much I appreciated him through the pack bond. *Thank you for all you have done for me, and for Sterling. I look forward to getting to know you better.* I held him at arm's length, making him meet my eyes. He dipped his head once, acknowledging he had gotten my message.

I laced my fingers through Sterling's and looked into his eyes. "Let's go home."

EPILOGUE

STERLING

SIX MONTHS LATER

*T*HE MAIN HOUSE was overflowing with pack members, cubs, friends, and best of all laughter. There was a joy about the pack that had been missing for years. Mack and Casey had made it back with their cubs. Rook and Jasmine were cuddled up on a wicker loveseat. Seeing how she was more comfortable with the physical contact he poured on her made me smile. They had really worked on their relationship and putting her demons to rest. Marla was there with the two cubs she had brought back to foster, though I had a feeling adoption would soon be in the future.

Gazing out over all of this were Jerome and Susanne, content and happy at last. I was sure that being grandparents had a lot to do with that. I searched the crowd and found Reana sitting with Marla and playing with the cubs. She had taken a quick connection with the boy, Felix, and his inner fox. She spent time with him daily between her shifts at the Silver Fox and her time at home with me. It was good for them both, and put an ache in my chest. I hated to let her down, and today was not the day for that. Today was for celebration.

Leo and Wyatt had even shown up to celebrate the day with us. This was the first pack celebration in over fourteen years. We were long overdue.

"Hey there, I wondered when you would show up." Reana wrapped her arms around me. I hadn't noticed her move from Marla's side. "How did the doctor's appointment go?"

I held her to me "It went fine, we can talk about it later tonight." I tried to keep the sadness from my voice, but she was a keen one.

"Not good eh, you know it's ok either way. I love you no matter what." She stood on tiptoe to kiss me.

"Ray Ray, come play!" Felix called out to her. I gazed down and smiled.

"Go, we'll have time later." I urged her forward and went to sit with Jerome and Suzanne.

"It's good to see you so happy, Sterling," Suzanne greeted, hugging me.

"You deserve it, my friend," Jerome agreed. "Come have a seat and enjoy the happiness around us." I pulled a chair up and sat next to him. "Now tell me what's bothering you. Today is a day of celebration, and you look like you have a black cloud hanging over you." Jerome leaned in and using his Alpha magic, created it so no one else would hear the words we exchanged. I followed Reana as she played with Felix and his litter mate Fiona.

"You know I had that appointment today, right?'

"Yes, but I thought it was just a checkup," Jerome replied.

"It was, but they decided to do a little more testing. Rea and I have been trying to get pregnant but haven't been lucky. Reana thought it was her so she went to the pack doctor. She checked out perfectly healthy and able to carry cubs." I breathed deep. "She said we just needed to stop worrying and let it happen, I wasn't so sure. She doesn't know that I had them test me during my yearly checkup, the results came back that I'm sterile. We can't have cubs because of me, Jerome, and I don't know how to tell her. I don't want to break her heart, she was so looking forward to being a mom." I rambled it all out.

"Sterling, we've been friends for many years. How many times have you over worried about situations? Look at her, your Reana. She is a strong woman, and an even stronger mate. She may be sad for a short time, but you must know she will never blame you." Jerome paused.

Suzanne chose that moment to poke her nose in. "I know you boys are in your secret talk bubble, but you know I hear everything through the mate bond. I just want to say one thing, there's a cub right out there that needs parents of its own kind. Those cubs together are becoming more than Marla can handle, and she has no experience teaching a fox how to be a fox. Think about that. You and Reana have a family just waiting for you in that child."

Jerome kissed his mate. "My mate always comes up with the best compromises. Go sit with your mate and get to know Felix. When you talk with her tonight, be open to talking about adopting him. I know she will be."

I spent the rest of the afternoon with my mate playing with Felix, eating, and relaxing with the rest of my family after he passed out from exhaustion. Yes, I could see that little spitfire in our home. He was a prankster, and made me remember what it was like to be so young and carefree.

As the day turned to night and the destruction we caused during the celebration was cleaned up I took Rea's hand. "Will you walk with me?"

"Always."

We walked in companionable silence for a few minutes before she stopped and pulled me to face her.

"Now tell me what's going on. I can feel the wall you put up and I've been calm about it all day, but now it's time to take it down. Sterling, you know you can tell me anything."

She was right and she would love me no less because of it. Scraping the courage together I told her what the doctor shared with me earlier and then waited for her response.

"Oh, babe, I'm so sorry." Her eyes filled with tears and my heart broke, until I realized they weren't tears for her, they were for me. She showered me with love and warm understanding and comfort through our mate bond letting me know she was sad, yes, but okay. "I know we wanted cubs of our own, but I still have you, and that's really all I need."

"I really don't deserve you, my little fox." I pulled her into me and held her, absorbing her love and warmth, returning the joy I felt at just having her as my mate. I chose that time to spring Suzanne's idea on her. "You know, we may still be able to have a family."

"How?" She leaned back a bit and questioned me with her eyes.

"Suzanne suggested that we adopt Felix. Marla has done a wonderful job with him, but now that he and Fiona have adapted to the pack they are becoming a handful for her. Not that she will ever admit that, but Felix is at an age he needs parents or guardians of his own species. I've seen how you are with him, you two have developed your own special bond already."

"We have, but what does Marla think about this? She loves those cubs more than life itself. Do you think she'd be willing to give him up?"

"If it's to us I think so. We would have to word our proposition carefully. But first, why don't we see if Felix wants to have a sleepover, sort of a test run? We can see how things go from there."

"Oh yes!" Reana's excitement vibrating through her. "Come on, let's go find them." She pushed out of my arms and skipped back to the yard looking for Marla and Felix. "Marla! Hey, wait up!"

I hurried to catch up with them, finding a frazzled Marla trying to coral two cranky cubs refusing to go home.

"What, Reana?" she snapped.

"Looks like you've got your hands full there. Let me help," I offered, reaching to take a squirming Felix out of her left arm so she could wrap both arms around an almost asleep Fiona. "What would you say to only having one cranky cub tonight?"

"I would say that would be heaven, but it's not nice to tease like that."

"We aren't," Reana chirped. "What if Felix had a sleepover with us?"

Marla looked between us a bit skeptical and spoke next through the pack bonds. *Sterling, are you sure about that? He can be a handful.*

I smiled and responded, *I'm sure, actually never more so, and you know he and Reana have a bond that goes deeper than just playmates. Let us take him off your hands, if just for a night.*

I could see the wheels turning in Marla's head until everything clicked into place. *This isn't going to be for just one night, is it? Suzanne put the same idea into your head that she's been wrapping into mine. She thinks you two would be better parents than I.*

Uh oh, this wasn't going quite as I had

planned. "No, it's just for tonight. I would never take a cub from you. Yes, Suzanne spoke to me but the decision is not one she can make, or that we can make. Let him sleep over and we'll bring him home after you get off work tomorrow. We can talk more then.

Marla visibly relaxed. "I'm sorry, guys, I didn't mean to be snippy. I'm running on about ten hours of sleep in the last ten days. If Felix would like to sleep over it's fine with me."

"Yay!" Felix shouted "Sleep over with Rea Rea!"

We all laughed at his excitement. Marla hugged Reana and then me. "We'll talk more tomorrow, he does need you guys in his life, and we can figure out the logistics. For now enjoy his little sneaky side and let me warn you to hide your phones, he's a genius with cracking passwords and loading really annoying alarms and ringtones." She turned and carried Fiona off towards her house, exhaustion dragging her steps, and I hoped that tonight she'd be able to get a good night's rest.

I hefted Felix onto my shoulders. "Okay big guy, rule number one, no phone pranks. Now let's go home for a hot chocolate night cap." Felix bounced in excitement.

"Oh boy, you get to stay up with him then when the sugar high kicks in." Reana laughed as she followed us her happiness radiating down our bond as her next words hit. *"May it be the first of many."*

Her words and Felix's excitement put a smile on my face I knew wouldn't fade for a very long time. For the first time in many years I prayed to the Fates. I prayed that they allowed us to become the parents I knew Felix needed, and allowed us to have the child we so desperately wanted.

THE END

ABOUT THE AUTHOR

MOTHER TO TWO boys, 3 four-legged babies, and wife to a loving husband who doesn't mind the extra voices in her head Miranda grew up on a dairy farm in Illinois, but calls Portland, TN home now. She is an avid reader, coffee addict, and loves her day job. Though her true passion is in creating her own worlds, characters, and stories for her readers.

Website: www.mirandalynn.com

Facebook www.facebook.com/MirandaLyn

Twitter: @MirandaLynnBks

Email: mirandalynnbooks@gmail.com